"My mom [...] **to be my f**[...] **the idea of moving in with me."**

"That's a lot to ask. I don't see why I should—"

"Did you like having sex with me?"

Heat rose to Val's face. And settled lower, too. "I— uh— suppose I—"

"Never mind." Teague smiled. "I know the answer."

"That was never the problem. The problem was—"

"Me getting serious. I'm aware. And I'm suggesting a reboot. A do-over. Sex without strings."

She took a shaky breath. "You're not capable of that."

"What if I give you my word? Ask anybody who knows me. My word is solid."

Oh, boy. She'd experienced first-hand how solid he could be. How hot. How creative...

"You're thinking about it."

"Am not."

"Are so. Your eyes just went dark green. That's a tell."

MARRIAGE-MINDED COWBOY

THE BUCKSKIN BROTHERHOOD

Vicki Lewis Thompson

Ocean Dance Press

MARRIAGE-MINDED COWBOY
© 2021 Vicki Lewis Thompson

ISBN: 978-1-63803-965-5

Ocean Dance Press LLC
PO Box 69901
Oro Valley, AZ 85737

This is a work of fiction. Any resemblance to actual persons, living or dead, business establishments, events, or locales is entirely coincidental.

Visit the author's website at
VickiLewisThompson.com

Want more cowboys? Check out these other titles by
Vicki Lewis Thompson

The Buckskin Brotherhood
Sweet-Talking Cowboy
Big-Hearted Cowboy
Baby-Daddy Cowboy
True-Blue Cowboy
Strong-Willed Cowboy
Secret-Santa Cowboy
Stand-Up Cowboy
Single-Dad Cowboy
Marriage-Minded Cowboy

The McGavin Brothers
A Cowboy's Strength
A Cowboy's Honor
A Cowboy's Return
A Cowboy's Heart
A Cowboy's Courage
A Cowboy's Christmas
A Cowboy's Kiss
A Cowboy's Luck
A Cowboy's Charm
A Cowboy's Challenge
A Cowboy's Baby
A Cowboy's Holiday
A Cowboy's Choice
A Cowboy's Worth
A Cowboy's Destiny
A Cowboy's Secret
A Cowboy's Homecoming

1

His mom's ringtone. Teague Sullivan tucked his just-opened bottle of hard apple cider in the fridge and reached for his phone on the kitchen counter. "Hey, Mom!"

She usually called on Sunday toward the end of the day and that worked for him, too. Once he'd brought the horses in from the pasture and distributed hay flakes, he had his evenings to himself. All to himself, lately.

"Teague, I've just had the most incredible idea."

"What's that?" He wandered out to the front porch of his little house to check on the August sunset. Some plump cumulous clouds could turn it into a beauty. The view from his place was almost as good as the one from his boss's up on the hill.

"I've decided I should move to Montana."

"What?"

"Move. To. Montana."

"But... but Oregon's your home." He scrambled to make sense of it. "Your stomping grounds. Your sister's there, and all your friends."

"And my only child lives in Montana. You're lonely out there. I can tell."

"Mom, I'm not lonely." Was *she* lonely? Unlikely. Something else was going on.

"You can't fool me. There's a sad note in your voice. I've been hearing it all summer. I've made up my mind, so there's no use trying to change it. I've already contacted a rental agent."

"In Apple Grove? Do we have any?" The town seemed too small to support one.

"I meant I contacted a rental agent in Eugene. She'll take care of finding a suitable tenant for my house. I considered selling, but renting it would give me an income stream, so I—"

"You're very sweet to consider moving here, but I'm not lonely and it makes no sense for you. While I'd love to have you nearby, I can't have you uprooting—"

"Nonsense. It's not uprooting, it's repotting in a new location where I'm meant to be. Montana's beautiful. I've checked into getting my teaching credentials accepted over there and it looks doable."

"But even if you get certified, the substitute jobs will go to the teachers who retired from the Apple Grove District, not a retiree from Oregon."

"At first, maybe, but I'll make friends and eventually work my way in."

He didn't doubt it. She had the tenacity of a mountain goat. "But you're involved in so many things — the clothing drive, the literacy program, the Tottering Tappers. You can't leave that dance group. You're the glue holding it together."

"You're more important than any of that. Luckily, you and I get along great. We like the same TV shows and the same kind of food. We can share the household chores just like we did when you were living at home. It'll be—"

"Hold on." Tension gripped the back of his neck and traveled around to his temples, creating a dull ache that promised to get worse. "You're planning to live with *me*?"

"Of course, silly! You have that cute little two-bedroom house and I've always wanted to live on a ranch. Thanks to all the time I've spent at Julie and Steve's operation, I can help you with the horses. I can—"

"I'm afraid there's a problem."

"What kind of problem?"

"Not a problem, really. Good news." He had seconds to concoct a lie big enough to derail her plan. He loved her. That didn't mean he wanted her living in his house.

"Oh? What news?"

"We were planning to make the call together, but we've been so busy we—"

"*We*? Who's *we*?"

"My fiancée." He gulped. "I'm engaged." Closing his eyes, he sucked in a breath as she went bananas on the other end of the line.

He'd lied to his mother before. What kid hadn't? But never about something so major. Then again, some circumstances required the nuclear option.

Eventually she settled down enough to pepper him with questions. "Who is she? How did you meet? When did you ask her? Have you bought a ring? When's the—"

"It literally just happened." Five seconds ago, to be exact. Val would have a conniption fit when he told her what he'd done.

"I didn't know you were serious about someone."

He winced at the hurt in her voice. "It's complicated. I asked her back in June, but she needed to think about it. I didn't want to get your hopes up." Semi-true.

"She had to think about it for two months?"

"Yes, ma'am." They'd been forced to see each other twice a week for riding lessons, giving them a constant reminder of that fateful night when she'd flatly refused to marry him. Guaranteed she'd thought about it.

"I can't imagine why she'd have to debate the issue. You're a great catch."

"She was afraid we were rushing into it." Understatement of the year. "We hadn't dated for very long." One week. "We know each other much better, now." Sure did, and he fully understood the colossal blunder he'd made with his premature proposal.

"I take it you're living together."

"Um, yes." She lived in his heart. Did that count?

"What's her name?"

"Valerie. Valerie Jenson."

"What does she look like?"

"Tall, slender, blonde." Sexy. Funny. Smart.

"That's your type, all right. I suppose she has blue eyes, too." His mom was still miffed that he'd left her out of the loop. Good thing he had.

"Green, although if she wears something blue, they seem blue. But when she has on green, then they're absolutely green."

"If you've paid that much attention to her eye color, you're definitely smitten."

"Yes, I am." Sad to say.

"I'm excited for you, son. Looks like I don't have to worry about you being lonely."

"No, ma'am."

"I'll table my plan of moving out there for now. On the other hand, it worries me a little that she didn't jump at the chance to marry you."

"She has her reasons. Her older sister married too soon, had a couple of kids and got divorced. Val doesn't want to follow in her footsteps."

"But now she's convinced you two are right for each other?"

"Love's a powerful motivator."

"Now I understand that sad note I've heard in your voice all summer. You were in limbo."

"Uh-huh."

"Do you want to bring her here or should I drive over there?"

Should've seen that coming. "Well, I—"

"The sooner, the better. Now that I'm not moving, I'll get back on the substitute list. School will be starting here before you know it."

Bingo. Perfect excuse. "Same here, and Val's a fourth-grade teacher. She'll—"

"A teacher? That's fabulous!"

"It is, except the timing isn't great since she'll be busy getting organized for the first week of—"

"Or it could be the perfect time. We can get acquainted while I help her with bulletin boards and stuff. See if that appeals to her."

Foiled again. "I'll ask."

"I'll bet she'll go for it. And even if she doesn't, I doubt she'll be *that* busy. Unless it's her first year there?"

"No, she's been at the school for... several years." Sad that he didn't know how many.

"Does she know I'm a retired teacher?"

"I'm sure I've mentioned it." If not, it would be first on his list when he threw himself on her mercy.

"I'm delighted we have that in common. I'd love to see how she sets up her classroom. I miss doing that. Talk to her and see what she says."

"Okay." It would be some talk, all right. He might not come out of it alive.

"If she's not open to that, I'll spend whatever time I can with her. Obviously, I can't stay with you, but Ed might not mind if I bunked at her house for a few nights."

"You know she'd be fine with it." No point in putting up roadblocks to that suggestion. His boss and his mother had bonded from her first visit eight years ago and they'd become better friends with each trip since.

Maybe if she stayed in the big house with Ed, and Val agreed to masquerade as his fiancée for a few days... oh, hell, who was he kidding? Val would hate this. Once he made his insane request, she'd kick his ass right out.

"Be sure and tell her what a good teacher I am."

"Don't worry, I will."

"Call me back when you've checked with Ed and Valerie. Don't try to call me tonight, though. I'm going over to Beth Ann's. The Tappers are gathering for another one of her parties. I can't remember exactly what she's selling this time. The company's name is *Fun in the Sack.*"

"Mom."

"Did I shock you?" She sounded amused.

"It's not that. I just—"

"Oh, relax. It's probably a clever play on words and not what you're thinking. But if it is what you're thinking, I'll buy a few things for Valerie's bridal shower. Talk soon! Love you!" She disconnected.

He'd lay money his mom was heading off to a sex toys party. He wouldn't put anything past that bunch of ladies. His mom was a lot of fun. That's why Ed liked her. Val would, too, under different circumstances.

He stared at the brilliant array of red, orange and pink clouds to the west. The reflection lit up the mountain range to the east, bathing the slopes with the same warm colors. Stunning.

Back in June, while Ed was off competing in a barrel racing event in Wyoming, Val had spent the weekend at the ranch. They'd watched a sunset like this one and made love on the porch as the light faded. Perfect.

A week later, he'd blown the program to smithereens. But until then, she'd had a good time. They could have a good time again, this time with firm ground rules. No proposal. No declarations of love. Just amazing sex. Would she go for it?

Only one way to find out. He made the call.

"Hi, Teague."

"Hey, Val. Listen, I have a favor to ask."

"What?"

"I'd rather ask it in person. Is there any chance I could drop by?"

"Now?"

"Now would be good, but if that's not convenient, I can—"

"You might as well come over now. The riding lesson isn't optimal for having a personal conversation."

"That's why I called, so I could get this done before tomorrow."

"I'll see you, soon, then."

"Thanks. I'm on my way." He disconnected. Then he ran a hand over his jaw. Five o'clock shadow. No time to shave.

Might be better if he showed up scruffy. Any attempt to impress her would be counterproductive.

Somehow he'd convince her he'd completely lost the urge to get hitched. *Fun in the sack.* That's all it could be — a game to keep his mother from moving in.

2

Valerie's case of nerves was frustrating. She'd interacted with Teague twice a week for the past two months and she'd eventually achieved a state of calm detachment. The Monday and Thursday riding lessons at the Buckskin didn't faze her anymore.

But during those lessons, she and Teague had been surrounded by chaperones — four mischievous girls who'd soon be in her fourth-grade class, plus her teaching buddy Nell, and Nell's fiancé Zeke. Evidently those folks helped keep her steady, because the prospect of facing Teague alone had turned her into a hot mess.

She'd fussed with her hair, put on lipstick and straightened the living room. She'd almost changed out of her old pair of shorts and ratty t-shirt.

Fighting that impulse, she walked around the room turning on lights. It wasn't dark enough yet to require all that wattage, but she craved operating room glare. Her house couldn't look the least bit romantic. Or sexy.

The rumble of his truck gave her heart palpitations. She hadn't closed the curtains in the living room for fear it would add a cozy vibe. That meant dashing into the kitchen so he wouldn't see her hanging out in the living room waiting for his knock.

When it came, she jumped. Damn it! She didn't want him to know how agitated she was. Forcing herself to stay put, she drew in two slow, deep breaths. Then she sauntered to the door and opened it.

Why did he have to look so good? It wasn't like he'd dressed up. He still had on his work clothes — his favorite Stetson, snug t-shirt and wear-softened jeans.

He hadn't shaved, either. His casual presentation stirred memories of their hot weekend at the ranch. What they'd worn had been less important than how easily it could be stripped off.

"Thanks for seeing me."

"You made it sound important." Had he always been this tall?

"It is important. Can I come in?"

"Yes, of course." She stepped back. "Did you get new boots?"

"No, ma'am. Same ones." He walked through the doorway, filling the space with his broad shoulders. "Why?"

"You just seem… taller."

"Guess the growth hormones have kicked in."

"Seriously? You're taking—"

"I'm teasing."

"Oh." She closed the door and the soft click sounded way too intimate. The last time he'd stepped into her house they'd… *don't go there.* "Can I get you something to drink?"

"No, thanks." He took off his hat and ran a hand through his hair. "But maybe we should sit down."

"All right." She gestured to the couch, their first make-out spot. "Have a seat." She took the chair across from it. A coffee table separated them, an extremely flimsy barrier.

He sat with his knees slightly apart, his hands resting on the faded denim covering his thighs, his hat beside him. He rubbed his palms back and forth a couple of times. Clearly he was nervous, too. "I don't know where to start."

"Teague, if this is about what happened in June, we've been over all—"

"This is something new. My mother called tonight."

Oh, no. He and his mom were close. "Is she okay? Is anything—"

"She's fine. Eager to start substitute teaching again when the school year begins. Did I tell you she's doing that now that she's retired?"

"You did."

"Good. I couldn't remember if I had. She's a great teacher. I'm glad she didn't completely hang it up."

"I'm sure her district is glad, too." Strangest conversation ever. If he started talking about the weather she'd—

"I told her we were engaged."

She shot out of the chair. "You *what?*"

"It was the first thing I—"

"Are you *nuts*?"

"I had to do something fast." Grabbing his hat, he stood. "That's what popped into my head when she announced that she was coming to live with me because I sounded lonely and I can't imagine having her living with—" He gulped for air. "This was the only way to—"

"Time out." What a doofus. "Do you have your phone?"

"I do, but—"

"Call her back. Tell her you misspoke."

"I can't call her. She's at a sex toys party."

"*Huh*?"

"It might not be sex toys, but it's one of those home party things where you invite your friends and sell stuff and it's called *Fun in the Sack* and I know those ladies so I'll bet you anything—"

"Call her anyway!" She gave her arm a quick pinch. Yep, this was real. "If she doesn't pick up, leave a message."

"But I—"

"You have to set the record straight ASAP. Or next thing you know she'll book a flight and throw me a bridal shower."

"She'd probably drive."

"I don't give a hoot if she shows up on the back of an elephant! Call her and stop the crazy train!"

"Okay." He pulled out his phone. Then he shoved it back in his pocket. "But first I have something to say."

"*You* have something to say? Buster, I have an entire speech on the tip of my tongue. But I'm holding my fire until after you make that call." She crossed her arms.

"Val, hear me out. Please."

She met his gaze. That intense look of his still got to her. She'd been avoiding direct eye contact ever since he'd walked through the door. But his heartfelt *please* had coaxed her into turning her head and there it was — her kryptonite. "Talk."

"I'm not the same guy I was back in June."

No, you're even sexier. "Funny, but you look a lot like him. Same hat, same boots." *Same muscles that make me want to give you a long, slow chest massage.*

"I got caught up in marriage mania. Seemed like every five minutes somebody at the Buckskin was getting engaged."

"I wouldn't know."

"Take my word for it. I've been hanging with that bunch for years. Nobody was talking about getting married. Then boom, everyone was into it. I let myself get swept up in their deal. Thank you for slapping some sense into me."

"I did *not* slap you, although I was tempted."

"You probably should have after I hounded you to see things my way. And in the process, I ruined a good thing." His voice grew husky. "A very good thing."

A shiver ran up her spine. He used to have that same throaty murmur after they'd had sex. Fantastic sex. "And your point is?"

"My mom wants to meet you. If you'd pretend to be my fiancée when she's here, she'll drop the idea of moving in with me."

"That's a lot to ask. I don't see why I should—"

"Did you like having sex with me?"

Heat rose to her face. And settled lower, too. "I— uh— suppose I—"

"Never mind." He smiled. "I know the answer."

"That was never the problem. The problem was—"

"Me getting serious. I'm aware. And I'm suggesting a reboot. A do-over. Sex without strings."

She took a shaky breath. "You're not capable of that."

"What if I give you my word? Ask anybody who knows me. My word is solid."

Oh, boy. She'd experienced first-hand how solid he could be. How hot. How creative...

"You're thinking about it."

"Am not."

"Are so. Your eyes just went dark green. That's a tell."

"Just because I'm thinking about it doesn't mean I have any intention of—"

"Why not? Isn't that what you're looking for? A carefree romp with a guy who won't get mushy?"

Her stupid heart was pounding at the prospect. What was the hitch? "I thought you wanted your mom to believe we're engaged."

"I do."

"Engaged people say mushy things to each other. Zeke and Nell do it all the time."

"What I say in public will just be part of the charade. What I say in private is what counts. I doubt I'll be saying much at all. I'll be too busy making you—"

"Stop it." She whirled away from him as a fresh wave of heat flowed through her. "No fair."

"Val, there's no downside to this." His voice was like velvet. "You can test me during my mom's visit. If I fail the test, which I won't, just walk away. Except I'd appreciate it if you stick with the program until she leaves. Once she does, disaster averted. She won't be looking to move once the school year starts."

Dear God, she was weakening. She turned back to him. "She'll want to hear about our wedding plans."

"I told her you needed two months to decide before you accepted my proposal, so—"

"She doesn't know our history?"

"No, which turns out to be a good thing. Anyway, she thinks you live with me so you'd need to move in. We both know what will happen if we're alone in that house overnight, so why not enjoy ourselves?"

Her body said *yes* while her head said *are you an idiot?* "Two months ago you wanted to marry me. Now you want a pretend engagement. You'll sink into marriage mode in no time."

"Exactly the opposite. After what happened in June, there's no way I'll go there. But I sure miss what we had together. It was good, Val. Really good." That slow smile turned her inside out.

"I never denied that, but—"

"Then give me another shot."

"What about our supposed wedding plans?"

"A long engagement makes sense after you took two months to decide. She knows you're cautious about this."

"She'd be right."

"If I tell her not to pester us to name a date, she won't."

"Is there an end game?"

He shrugged. "We're not committing to anything. Eventually it could just fizzle out on its own."

"Maybe." More likely it would blow up like last time. He wasn't a *fizzle out* kind of guy.

"Meanwhile, I'll have breathing room, time to gently coax my mom to stop worrying about my future."

There had to be a catch. She'd better locate it before he seduced her into going along with this nonsense. If he invited her into the bedroom he'd make his case for sure.

"Anyway, that's my pitch. Take some time to think about it."

"Really?" She blinked. Why hadn't he pressed his advantage?

"Yes, ma'am. Seems only right."

"But what if your mom—"

"She won't head over here until I say the word." He put on his hat and tugged the brim low over his eyes. "But if you could let me know before the riding lesson tomorrow, that would be helpful."

Her breath caught. He'd never looked more manly, his hat pulled low to shade his eyes and his scruff giving him an edginess that dampened her panties. She clenched her fists to keep from grabbing him and hauling him to bed.

She cleared her throat. "I'll contact you before then."

"Thanks." Touching two fingers to the brim of his hat, he walked out the door without looking back.

Whew. The Teague who'd proposed in June was not the Teague who'd just left. She wanted this one. She wanted him bad.

3

By riding into the sunset when Val clearly wanted a kiss and possibly more than a kiss, Teague acted on instincts he'd never used. His previous approach to women had been uncomplicated. He'd worn his heart on his sleeve.

But that behavior had netted him a painful rejection back in June. Time to change tactics. Had he intrigued her? Or had he given her an opening to scamper away? Who knew? But he couldn't do much worse than he had in June. Now he was in wait-and-see mode.

Back at his place, he made himself some dinner, cleaned up the dishes and carried another bottle of cider out to the porch. A few stars had popped out in the navy sky. Should he fetch his harmonica?

Nah. He was too agitated to do that instrument justice tonight. Boots propped on the railing, he glanced up at the lighted windows of the big house on the hill.

His boss — Edna Jane Vidal, better known as Ed — could be entertaining some of the Babes on Buckskins, a competitive barrel racing group. Henri Fox, owner of the Buckskin Ranch and a member of the Babes, was his connection with the Buckskin Brotherhood. Best buddies a guy could have.

His claim to Val, that he'd been caught up in the recent marriage frenzy gripping the Brotherhood, had a smidgen of truth to it. But he'd fallen hard for that woman and his devotion had only deepened over the summer. His feelings went beyond any copycat behavior.

Did she suspect? He'd done his best to hide his feelings tonight. If she agreed to his plan, he'd continue that trajectory. Wouldn't be easy, but if it prevented his mom from becoming his roommate—

Headlights. Probably someone going to see Ed. Or not. The headlights passed the big house and made the turn toward his cabin. His chest tightened. The distinctive sound of a V-6, the motor in Val's little pickup, kicked his pulse into high gear.

He set his half-full bottle on the porch floor and swung his booted feet off the railing. She wouldn't have driven out here to tell him she wasn't interested. His heart pumped faster as he descended the steps.

Slow down, boy. He planted his feet at the bottom of the steps. Rushing over to open her door and help her out would send the wrong message.

The arousing beat of Luke Bryan's *Country Girl* poured out the open window of her cab as she drove in, headlights on high beam pointed right at him. He tugged his hat down to block the glare as she braked about five yards away.

Leaving the lights and the music on, she climbed out, her body moving to the rhythm. When she stepped into the spotlight, the breath left his lungs. She danced toward him wearing a filmy red dress. And nothing underneath.

He began to shake and sweat. His cock thickened as she wiggled her hips and spread her arms to add a shimmy to the mix. She was coming for him.

About four feet away, she continued to tempt him with her sexy dance as she gave him a once-over, her gaze lingering on his fly. A slow smile spread over her rosy lips. "Want some of this, cowboy?"

"Yes, ma'am." His voice rasped. "I surely do."

"Tell you what." She ran her tongue over her lips. "I'll go inside and make myself comfy while you tend to my truck. Then you can come tend to me."

"Got it."

She swirled past him, the scent of her perfume mingling with the aroma of hot woman. Clearly this maneuver had turned her on, too.

Ignoring the pain in his crotch, he crossed quickly to the pickup and cut the engine and lights. Luke Bryan's song stayed in his head as he shoved the truck door closed and hobbled back to the house.

The living room was dark, the way he'd left it, but light spilling from his bedroom doorway was enough to see the boots she'd left by the door and the red dress tossed over the back of the couch.

He sent his hat sailing in the same direction and pulled his T-shirt over his head while nudging off his boots. By the time he reached the bedroom, he'd unbuckled and unzipped.

She'd tossed the covers back and piled the pillows against the headboard. Lounging against them in all her naked glory, she inspired a surge of lust so strong he almost came. "I take it we have a deal?"

"Depends." She held his gaze. "How do you like the tone I've set tonight?"

"I like it fine."

"Think you can maintain it?"

"Oh, yeah."

"Then take off those Wranglers, cowboy. Let's get this par—" Her breath hitched. "Oh, my. I'd forgotten how well-endowed you are."

He kicked away his jeans and walked toward the bed. "Then allow me to refresh your memory."

"I do believe I will." She scooted over to make room. "Bring that bad boy down here. I'd like to—"

"Not this time." He yanked open the bedside drawer. Still a few little raincoats left in there. He'd replenish the supply tomorrow. "After that dance routine, I have business to transact with you, lady." He ripped open the package and rolled on the condom.

"Are you taking charge?"

"Yes, ma'am." Climbing into bed, he straddled her, cupped her face in both hands and kissed those saucy lips until she began to moan and dig her fingers into his backside.

He lifted his mouth a fraction from hers. "Slide that sweet tush down so I can get some traction."

She wiggled into position and he moved between her thighs, his brain a lava field, his groin so taut he feared an instant explosion. Centering his cock, he drove deep, just in case he lost control.

He didn't, but she did, arching upward and yelling his name. He milked the moment, thrusting fast and treating her to another orgasm before he ran out of room and surrendered to an epic climax. He made noise. Lots of it.

When the roaring in his ears eased up, he opened his eyes and checked to see how she was doing. Pretty good, judging from her pink cheeks and sparkling eyes. God, she was beautiful.

Couldn't say that, though. He cleared his throat. "Was that the tone you were looking for?"

"Sure was." Her voice was breathy. "Did you have fun?"

"Big fun."

"Excellent. Now let me up, please. I'm going home."

"Home?" True, she hadn't asked him to fetch her overnight bag when he switched off the truck. But they'd only had a taste just now. He'd assumed she'd stay and—

"You said you wanted a reboot. That's what tonight was all about, making sure we're on the same page. And in all honesty, after our conversation tonight, I was a wee bit... frustrated."

"Better now?"

"Much. Thank you."

"There's more where that came from."

"Don't I know it. I remember your amazing stamina. But seriously, I should go home. We've established ground rules and we've had an excellent reboot. I feel more confident this could work, but let's not push our luck."

Let's do. But she had a point. If they made love again so soon he might accidentally say something that would wreck the whole program. He was still learning the ropes. "You're right." He gave her a quick kiss and left the bed. "But don't leave until I have a chance to pull on my pants."

"I won't."

Damn, he *really* didn't want her to leave. But he couldn't let on. He washed up as quickly as possible and returned to the bedroom. She wasn't there. "Val?"

"Out on the porch."

He tugged on his briefs and jeans before walking barefoot through the darkened living room. Her boots and dress were no longer there and the porch light was off.

He stepped through the open door. She was waiting for him in the shadows, her hips propped against the railing as she faced him. A cool breeze brushed his sweaty chest and he shivered.

Don't go. He swallowed the words. "We need a plan."

"I figured. Let's start with this. Can we ditch the engagement ring routine?"

"I guess. But I don't know how—"

"We could tell your mom we're having it custom made."

"Sure. That works."

"In fact, let's say we've only told a few close friends and we're waiting until the ring is finished before going public."

He nodded. "And if she asks about this mythical ring, we can have the mythical designer run into glitches."

"You've got the idea." She hesitated. "Please tell me you don't have one tucked away. From before."

"No, ma'am. I might have been stupid to propose so quick, but I wasn't completely clueless. I knew you'd want to help choose it. I mean, if you'd said yes."

"Which I would. If I'd said yes."

Ouch. This conversation wasn't nearly as much fun as they'd had back in the bedroom.

She cleared her throat. "How soon will your mom show up?"

"If I give her the word tomorrow, she'll be here by Wednesday afternoon at the latest." Meeting her gaze, he curbed the urge to move within touching distance. Seemed wiser to avoid body contact when he still craved her.

"When do you want me to bring some of my stuff over?"

"Your choice."

"I'll do it Tuesday night, then."

"Not tomorrow night?" *Watch the hopeful tone, buddy*.

"Monday nights I have a standing date with Nell. It's our girl time now that she's living at the ranch instead of a few blocks away. I plan to fill her in on this development."

"Understood. I'll contact Zeke tomorrow and have him pass the word to the Buckskin gang."

"But not Claire."

"Right. Not Claire." He rubbed the back of his neck. "I hadn't thought about her and her three friends. Can we keep them out of this?"

"We have to try. We only have two lessons and the performance on Saturday. What if you tell your mom that we haven't mentioned the engagement to the kids because they'd get excited and it would distract them from doing their best on Saturday?"

"She might buy that."

"I think she will. She's a teacher. We're all about keeping our students focused."

"I'll ask Ed to reinforce that idea from a riding teacher's perspective. Mom will be staying up at the house with her."

"They get along?"

"Like a house afire. Ed looks forward to her visits."

"Will Ed be upset that we're fooling her with this fake engagement?"

"I don't think so. She's fond of my mother, but she'll be on my side."

"What about the Buckskin gang?"

"I doubt anyone will have a problem with it."

She gazed at him in silence for a moment. "Is that because they'll expect a fake engagement will lead to—"

"Maybe." No maybe about it. They'd love this plan.

More silence. "Tell me the truth. Do you expect the same thing?"

Careful, dude. "I have no expectations. Well, except for lots of time in bed with you."

"To soften me up?"

"I gave you my word. No mushy declarations of love, no veiled references to a happily-ever-after."

"I'll believe it when I see it."

"You can still back out." He held his breath.

"I don't want to."

He exhaled. "Why not?"

"Two reasons. Making love with you is amazing."

Making love. He probably shouldn't put too much stock in her use of that phrase, but he liked hearing it. "What else?"

"I'm curious as to whether you can actually do this. If you can't, oh, well. But if you can, then we could have a very good time for... however long it lasts."

"Trust me, I can do this."

"If you say so."

"Count on it."

4

Val slept better Sunday night than she had in more than two months. Good lovemaking had that effect on her, especially when she was lucky enough to enjoy that activity with Teague Sullivan. For the first time since their breakup in June, she was looking forward to today's riding lesson.

Chauffeuring three of the girls out to the Buckskin twice a week had become her job after Nell moved to the ranch to be with Zeke and Claire. Val's pickup was small, but she could fit one kid in the front and two in the back.

They spent the drive discussing the rope tricks *Uncle* Teague was teaching them. It was an honorary title Claire used and her friends had permission to call him that, too. Teague had won the girls' hearts when he'd presented each of them with junior-sized ropes in their favorite colors.

Spending time with the adorable chatterboxes who would soon be her students was one of Val's rewards for tolerating an uncomfortable situation all summer. Learning to ride had been another.

Her bond with the girls and a new skill were hers to keep, even if her fling with Teague blew up after his mom left. Maybe it wouldn't, though.

His text this morning had been straightforward. Almost businesslike. His mom would arrive around noon on Wednesday. He'd prepped her about the custom ring and maintaining secrecy around the girls.

So far, so good. Val had answered him with equal efficiency. But his red truck sitting by the barn kicked her pulse into high gear.

Why wait until tomorrow night to move into his house? Nell wouldn't stay late. Packing up and driving to the ranch after Nell left was doable and Teague would certainly be glad to—

Nope. Bad idea. She'd set the tone last night. Rushing over there tonight would send the wrong signal. She'd leave the plan in place.

As she switched off the motor, Nell and Claire hurried out of the barn. Nell's dark hair was tamed into a single braid down her back. Claire sported an identical braid, only blonde. She looped a purple rope over her shoulder as she made a beeline for the truck.

Nell followed. Not smiling. She'd heard.

Riley grabbed her red rope from the floor of the front passenger seat, hopped out of the truck and flipped the seat back to let Piper out. Piper clutched her green rope and almost lost her glasses in her eagerness to climb down.

Val moved the driver's seat for Tatum, who jumped out holding fast to her blue rope. She dashed around the tailgate and headed for the other three.

Claire took charge, as usual. "I thought you guys would *never* get here. Come on." She started back toward the barn, moving fast. "I did the coolest thing with Lucky's mane. You'll love it!"

"Walk, girls!" Val called out automatically. She tucked her keys and purse under the seat and turned just as Nell rounded the back of the truck. Her expression said it all.

"You think I'm insane."

"Yep."

"It won't be like last time."

"Why not? You'll be his pretend fiancée. Before you know it, he'll be on bended knee begging you to make it real."

"He's promised he won't. He gave his word."

"Okay, maybe he won't actually propose, but you'll see it in his face. That's just as bad. It'll be déjà vu all over again, two miserable people who can't stand being in the same space."

"But we don't have to be in the same space. The riding demonstration on Saturday is the last time we need to see each other. If this turns out to be a disaster, we'll just go our separate ways."

"That's not so easy in a town the size of Apple Grove."

"Sure it is. Without the riding lessons, we might never have met."

"But now that you have a history with the guy, one you're about to embellish, you'll be looking for him around every corner."

"No, I won't."

"Really?" Nell crossed her arms and gave her the same look she used on misbehaving third-graders. "You stayed away from the Moose all summer because he might show up."

Hadn't thought of that. Damn.

"When you break up this time, and you will, it'll be ten times worse."

"But it doesn't *have* to go that way. He says he's not the same guy he was back in June. And maybe he's not. He didn't shave before he came over last night."

"I don't think I've ever seen an unshaven Teague."

"He says he was caught up in the marriage mania going on at the Buckskin, and he's over it."

Nell studied her. "I suppose there could be some truth to that. But I—"

"Don't worry. Even if he does go off the rails, I'm prepared to handle it."

"Are you? You'll have five days of close contact, and—"

"I can handle it, Nell."

"Hm." She didn't look at all convinced.

"Hey, did you and Zeke make good progress on the house this weekend?"

"We did. The Buckskin gang's pitching in, which means we might get it done before the wedding. Zeke's determined to carry me over the threshold whether the house is done or not."

Val smiled. "I predict it'll be done." She glanced toward the barn, where Teague would normally be conducting a roping lesson with the girls. The area was deserted. "Where is everybody?"

"Claire's probably teaching the girls how to braid a horse's mane. She did Lucky's before you got here. That's what she wanted to show them."

"Ah. Makes sense. Your matching hairstyles are cute as heck, by the way."

"Claire was the instigator. She thinks a single braid looks more cowgirl-ish. First I did hers and then I let her braid mine. Lucky was next on the list."

"I'll bet she wants to doll up the horses for Saturday."

"Definitely. Want to help?"

"You know it. I'm an excellent braider. We'll make those horses look—" Her brain shut down as Teague came through the barn door, a coiled rope over his broad shoulder and four adoring girls hanging on him like rock star groupies.

At a word from him, they let go and spread out, their excited voices tumbling over each other as he uncoiled his rope and began twirling it in a tight circle. The girls followed his lead, their colorful loops dancing in the same pattern as his.

"Want to head on over?"

"Sure." Heart thumping, she followed Nell around the back of the truck.

While continuing to twirl his rope, Teague glanced at her and smiled. "Hey, there, Miss Jenson."

"H—" She had to clear her throat before she could respond. "Hey there, Teague."

Nell gave her a look.

"Got a frog in my throat," Val muttered. On the way into the barn, she couldn't resist one more peek.

He met her gaze, winked and turned away.

She stumbled going into the barn. "Don't you dare say a word, Nell O'Connor. Once I get my sea legs, I'll be fine."

"I sure hope so, girlfriend."

5

Teague breathed deep in an attempt to settle down. Good thing he'd added a wink to that glance he'd given Val. He'd been fixated on her from the moment he'd walked out of the barn. He'd come so close to blowing his cover and it was only Day Two of the new program.

He continued the lesson, guiding the girls through the tricks they'd demonstrate on Saturday. Val and Nell led Butch and Sundance to the hitching post. As they groomed the horses, Zeke came out to chat with them. As if nothing had changed.

But everything had changed. Tomorrow night Val would move in with him. She'd share his bed, at least for the length of his mom's visit — Wednesday through Sunday. He'd tried to talk his mother into staying longer. She'd gently declined.

When the girls executed the routine with only a couple of minor mistakes, he coiled his rope. "Let's stop there. You're doing a terrific job." He collected the ropes from Piper and Tatum to store in the tack room until they left.

The girls followed him into the barn and Piper and Tatum split off to fetch Lucky and Prince from their stalls. The summer's lessons had turned those greenhorn girls into competent wranglers who could be trusted to handle the horses on their own. Gratifying.

Riley and Claire followed him into the tack room and Riley put her rope on the same shelf with Piper's and Tatum's. "Miss Jenson sure seemed happy while we were driving out here." She gave him a sly glance. "She was singing along with the radio."

That news cheered him up considerably. "I'm glad she's happy."

"I think she's getting interested in you again."

"Just because she was singing?"

"Also the way she looked at you a little while ago."

"I saw that, too." Claire hung her purple rope on a peg. "Do you still like her?"

"Yes."

"Then be careful. You don't want to mess up again."

"What do you mean?" God, he hoped these girls didn't know about his ill-fated proposal.

"You know, like trying to butter her up. Don't act like the teacher's pet."

Out of the mouths of babes.

"Claire's right." Riley shoved her hands in the back pockets of her jeans. "Miss Jenson's a little bit like my cat Bernice. If you try to pick her up, she runs away. But act like you don't care if she sits in your lap and she comes right over. My dog Jasper's the opposite. He's a lot like you, super friendly."

Claire nodded. "She's right. You and Jasper could be twins."

He ducked his head to hide a smile.

"Jasper's always trying to lick Bernice," Riley said. "If he'd just back off, she'd cuddle with him." She sighed dramatically. "Poor Jasper doesn't get it."

Teague turned his laughter into a cough. Riley was adorably serious. And incredibly wise. "You're saying I need to be less like Jasper?"

"Yes."

"But don't go too far." Claire faced him, her blue gaze earnest. "Jasper's a great dog. When he runs up to me all excited and happy, that makes me feel special."

"I appreciate the advice, ladies." They'd confirmed that he'd chosen the right path.

"You're welcome." Claire gave him a quick hug.

"And good luck." Riley held up her hand for a high five.

He smiled and tapped his palm against hers. "Thanks. I'll need it."

For the next hour, he monitored himself for any Jasper leanings when he interacted with Val. Achieving a balance between enthusiasm and reserve was tricky. His Jasper tendencies ran deep.

At the end of the lesson, Val asked the girls to wait in the truck while she had a word with him. First time she'd done that since the breakup. Could be good news or bad.

The girls answered *yes, Miss Jenson* in unison and all four hurried off, giggling. Nell and Zeke ducked into the barn.

Val walked toward him, her expression tough to read. Cold sweat trickled down his spine. She could still back out.

She met his gaze. "Nell thinks I'm making a serious mistake."

"She told me the same thing." He kept his tone casual. "What do you think?"

"After today's lesson, I'm ready to give it a shot if you are."

He let out a slow breath. "Okay, then."

"Were you hoping I'd change my mind?"

Hell, no. "Why do you ask?"

"You didn't smile as often today as you usually do. I wondered if you regretted asking me."

"No, ma'am." Evidently she was paying attention. Promising. "Just have a lot on my mind."

"That makes sense." She hesitated. "We didn't talk about what time I should drive over tomorrow evening."

"Whenever you want."

"No preference?"

He shrugged. "Not really."

"Then I'll be there by five so I can help you feed the horses."

"You don't have to—"

"I liked doing it when I was there before."

"No kidding? I thought you were just being nice."

"Nope."

A flicker of heat in her eyes jump-started his pulse. Was she remembering their hot make-session in the barn? "Then I'll meet you at my place at five."

"No need. I know where to find you. I'll park by the house and walk over."

I know where to find you. The slight huskiness in her voice gave her away. She was turned on. "All right."

"See you then."

"Yes, ma'am." He touched the brim of his hat and took a step back. The words *can't wait* almost slipped out.

"'Bye, Teague." A hint of a smile.

"'Bye, Val." He allowed himself a brief glance into her eyes. The air crackled and his jeans pinched. He turned and headed for the barn.

Nell lay in wait just inside the door. "Did she back out?"

"Sorry to disappoint you. She's still in."

"Doggone it, Teague. Can't you just tell your mother you don't want her to live with you?"

Zeke came out of the tack room. "That's a hard thing to say to your mom. In his shoes, I'm not sure I could have done it. Besides, Val's agreed to this."

"I know." Nell sighed.

Zeke put his arm around her shoulders. "She must think it's worth the risk. The rest of us do, too."

"But you guys didn't sit on the gazebo steps in the middle of the town square with Val while she sobbed her heart out."

"When was this?" Teague's gut twisted.

"The day after you two broke up. We met for lunch. And she'd kill me for telling you she was that upset, so please don't rat me out."

"I won't, but damn." He took off his hat and scrubbed his fingers through his hair. "I thought she was just ticked off. I didn't know—"

"Maybe they were mad tears," Zeke said.

Teague looked at him. "You didn't know about this incident, either?"

"Not until now. Could they have been mad tears, Nell?"

"A little bit, I guess, but she was devastated, too."

"I'll call it off." He crammed his hat on his head. "I'll give her time to get home and then I'll—"

"Don't be too hasty." Zeke gave Nell a squeeze and let go. "There's another way to look at this."

"No, there isn't. I thought I was just in danger of making her angry if I screwed up again, but if my actions could make her cry, then—"

"Then she's into you, buddy."

He stared at Zeke. "You think?"

"Ask Nell. She's the Valerie Jenson expert around here."

"Nell?"

She looked stricken.

"Nell, please."

"Maybe I was reading too much into it. Besides, that was then and this is now. She's had a whole summer to... I'm sure she's in a different place. It probably was mad tears. Yeah, now that I think about it, I'm—"

"Hey, everybody!" Claire charged through the door. "I couldn't figure out what happened to you guys. What are you all doing in here?"

"Loafing," Zeke said. "Sometimes wranglers need to relax, you know."

"Not me. I'm taking a rake and shovel out to the corral. Those horses left a few deposits." She grabbed her tools from the tack room. "Loaf on, dudes."

6

After Val dropped off the girls, she went home and phoned in the pizza order. Then she stripped down and took a quick shower to cool off. Once again, Teague's change of attitude had left her hot and bothered.

Clearly he'd dialed in a new program. No more adoring glances. Just brief eye contact that hinted at simmering lust. His slow-burn approach was driving her crazy.

She used to be able to read him, but now she couldn't tell what he was thinking. Mostly. That sizzling look he'd given her before he'd turned away had been clear enough.

Pulling on shorts and a T-shirt, she put her hair in a ponytail and shoved her feet into flip-flops. Soon the weather would be too cold for any of those things. Too cold for outdoor sex, too. Not yet, though. A flush of excitement warmed her all over.

Hey, girl, don't forget his mother will be on the premises. She kept leaving that factoid out of the equation. Not good.

How did a fiancée behave with a future mother-in-law, anyway? Nell had one. She should know. Maybe she'd have some tips on how to play the role. Or not, since she wasn't on board with Teague's scheme.

By the time the pizza arrived, Val had set the table, opened the wine and tucked it back in the fridge. Nell showed up five minutes later.

She came through the door holding a bakery box. "I picked up a pie from the Apple Barrel. It comes with my apologies."

"For what?"

"For second-guessing your decision. For acting like I know what's best."

"Aw, Nell. You're just worried about me. I get it."

She handed over the pie. "But who am I to say you're making a big mistake? I'm the only one in the Buckskin gang who thinks that, by the way."

Val led the way into the kitchen. "They don't know me like you do." She set the pie on the counter and opened the fridge to get the sauvignon blanc. "They're Team Teague, while you're the sole member of Team Val." She turned back to her with a smile. "Thank you for being my friend."

"Then as your friend, I need to ask you something."

"Okay." She crossed to the table and began pouring the wine. "What?"

"I'll wait until you've finished pouring."

"Must be a heavy-duty question." Placing the stopper in the bottle, she turned around.

"Kind of." She hesitated. "Is it possible you're in love with him?"

The question hung in the air, the question she'd asked herself a million times. "I am." She took a breath. "But not enough."

"You mean not enough to marry him?"

"Right. If I ever decide to marry a guy, and that's a big *if*, I need to be willing to give up all the things I like about being single."

"But you could gain so many other—"

"*You* can, Nell, because you've found someone you can't live without. I'm looking forward to the next few days with Teague, but if we decide to part ways after that, I'll survive just fine."

Nell gazed at her for a moment, then nodded. "Got it."

"Great. I'll stick this in the fridge and we can attack the pizza. I'm starving."

"Me, too." Nell pulled out the chair at what had become her designated spot and opened the box. "Yum. I— wait, why are there mushrooms? You don't much like—"

"But you do, so I decided—"

"You're supposed to get what you like when it's your turn to buy."

"And you splurged on an apple pie." She took her seat and lifted her wine glass. "I guess we were both feeling guilty."

"I definitely was. Here's to clearing the air." She tapped her wine glass against Val's.

"I'll drink to that." She took a mouthful of wine and let it slide over her tongue before she swallowed. "I like this one so much."

"We're serving it at the reception."

"Not apple cider? Doesn't that break some kind of town ordinance?"

"Almost, which is why we'll serve both wine and cider." Nell transferred a wedge of pizza to her plate. "Plus Ed's donating some of her pricey champagne. We'll have out-of-towners and not everyone's a fan of hard cider."

"I like it, but not as much as this. Or Ed's champagne." Setting down her glass, she scooped a slice of pizza out of the box. "Listen, I need some pointers on how future daughters-in-law are supposed to act."

"Like I'm supposed to know?"

"If you don't, I'm SOL. You're the only future daughter-in-law in my phone contacts."

"I doubt Teague's mother is anything like Zeke's."

"Probably not, but I'll bet there's some protocol." She bit into the pizza. The mushrooms weren't half-bad. Maybe her taste buds were changing.

"If there is, I've never heard of it. Just be nice to her." She finished her first piece and took a second.

"I'm not good at sucking up, if that's what you mean."

Nell shook her head, finished chewing and swallowed. "Sucking up could be a disaster. Teague's mom and Ed are buddies and Ed hates suck-ups. I assume Madeline does, too."

"Madeline? That's her name?"

"Teague didn't tell you?"

"We didn't get around to that."

Nell grinned. "I see."

"Okay, okay. We both went a little crazy Sunday night."

"You talked to him today, though."

"I did, but... this new version of Teague has me discombobulated."

"No, really?"

"Bite me."

Nell just smiled and took a sip of wine.

"Maybe I won't have to spend too much time with his mom."

Nell's snort of laughter made her choke on her wine. Grabbing her napkin, she put down her glass and dabbed at her eyes.

"What's so funny?"

"She's coming to meet *you*, girlfriend. You're the whole reason for the trip. She'll want to spend most of her visit with you."

"Well, she'll have to amuse herself on Friday. We have stuff to do."

"Teague hasn't mentioned that his mom wants to help get your room ready?"

She stared at Nell in dismay. "No, she can't! It's just you, me and the girls. I don't want Meredith or Marilyn or whatever her name is horning in on our special—"

"Madeline. And that's basically what I said to Teague, which is probably why he hasn't brought it up."

Val heaved a sigh. "I suppose an actual fiancée would be delighted to include her future mother-in-law."

"Yes, she would. Especially since this FMIL is an experienced elementary teacher. An actual fiancée would see it as a bonding opportunity."

"The fake fiancée sees it as a royal pain in the ass."

"I know." Nell gestured toward the pizza. "You take that bigger piece. Not as many 'shrooms."

"Okay, but I'm starting to like 'em." She picked up the larger of the two remaining pieces.

"Yeah? Does that mean we can have them every week?"

"Fine with me." She took a bite and chewed slowly. She'd so looked forward to spending Friday with the girls — working on both classrooms in the morning and taking them for a special lunch at the Moose afterward. "What if we come up with a reason to shift the classroom thing to Monday, after she's gone?"

"Riley's end-of-the-summer trip is next week. That's why we—"

"Damn, you're right."

"Hey, it won't be so bad. The girls won't mind. They love meeting new people, and Madeline clearly loves kids or she wouldn't be substituting after her retirement. Teague says she doesn't need the money. She donates a big chunk of it to her favorite charity."

"Hm." She took another bite, chewed and swallowed. "Nell, I just had an awful thought."

"Which is?"

"So far I've heard mostly good things about this woman. Inviting herself to live with Teague is a little out there, but otherwise, she sounds great. What if I like her? What if we like each other?"

"Then the next few days won't be as bad as you think."

"No, they'll be worse. I'll be tricking someone I like. I'm gonna hate that."

7

Usually by five in the afternoon, especially on warm days, Teague was sweaty and looking forward to a shower after he'd finished feeding the critters. Tonight he'd showered before feeding time. Silver, a white gelding and a former star in the world of trick riding, sniffed Teague's freshly laundered T-shirt.

"Not used to being served by such a sweet-smelling wrangler, are you, boy?" He dropped a hay flake into the net, taking his time because he'd promised Val she could help.

She'd be here any minute. That concept put his body on red alert, his heart pumping faster than normal and his skin flushed.

The soft rumble of her truck on the road sent a trickle of sweat down his spine. Would she drop off her stuff before walking to the barn? The house was unlocked, as usual, so she might choose to do that.

The thud of the truck's door made him catch his breath. The faint scratch of boots on dirt grew louder. *Not* putting her stuff in the house. Heading straight for the barn. Hot damn.

He concentrated on his breathing, going for a slow, steady rhythm. He'd partially achieved it when she appeared in the doorway, silhouetted against the warm glow of late afternoon sunshine. The light touched her blonde hair, creating a rim of gold around her head.

He fought the urge to go to her. Gripping the edge of the stall door to hold himself in place, he cleared his throat. "Hi, there."

"Hi, yourself." She glanced at the wheelbarrow loaded with hay flakes. "Looks like you started."

"Just did. Work gloves are in the tack room."

"I remember." Stepping into the barn, she ducked into the tack room and reappeared with the gloves. They were big on her, but she'd managed with them before. "Just hay flakes tonight?"

"That's it. They'll also get oats in the morning." The morning after they shared a bed the entire night. His groin throbbed.

"I want to help with that, too." A slight tremor in her voice betrayed her outward calm.

"Okay." Was she remembering what they'd done the last time they were alone in this barn?

"It seems like Ed doesn't have as many horses." Her color high, she surveyed the stalls on either side of the aisle.

Her blush gave her away. She was thinking about it just like he was. "Normally there would be one more. Ed trailered Cinnamon over to the Buckskin today so Claire could work him into the routine during Thursday's riding lesson."

"Good idea. I'll bet Claire's excited about that."

"Over the moon."

"But adding one more horse still wouldn't make the stable as full as I remember. Wasn't there a horse named Dusty? And another big brown one named... let me think... Hercules."

"Good memory. A kids' riding program wanted to expand and Ed gave them Dusty, Hercules and Jim."

"That was nice of her. I'm glad she didn't give them Nugget, though." She focused on the palomino three stalls down, who'd stuck his nose over the door to peer at her.

"Ed knows you're partial to him."

"But I never intended to come back here to ride, so why would she—"

"You'll have to ask her."

"Maybe I will." Banked heat flickered in her eyes. "What's her take on our... arrangement?"

He tightened his hold on the stall door. "She called it an *interesting development.*"

"Good description."

"Shall we get started?"

Her eyebrows rose.

His cock tried to do the same, but it was hampered by a layer of knit cotton and another of sturdy denim. "I mean with the feeding."

Her mouth curved in a smile as she glanced at the area below his belt buckle. "Tell that to your friend."

"My *friend* doesn't give a damn whether the horses get fed. But I do." He let go of the stall door and grasped the wheelbarrow handles. "Next stop, Toffee on the left and Nugget on the right. Take your pick."

"Nugget."

"Want to ride him tomorrow morning?"

"Depends."

"On what?"

"How often I ride you tonight."

He sucked in a breath. *Keep your cool, buddy. She's testing you. Play the game.* "I'll go easy on you, then. A morning ride would be nice."

"A midnight ride would be nice, too."

He dug deep, came up with a sexy reply. "Then I'll make sure we do both."

"I like the way you think."

Think? That skill was gone. She'd flash-fried his brain. He operated on auto-pilot, quickly stuffing the hay nets for Toffee and Herb, the ancient gelding Ed kept for sentimental reasons.

Val fed Nugget and Sir Eatsalot. "I'm glad Ed kept this guy, too."

"Nobody else would have that sway-backed food hog. Ed's promised him a home for the rest of his life."

"Your boss is a soft touch."

"Uh-huh." The words *soft* and *touch* coming out of her mouth weakened the fraying cord keeping his impulses in check. "We're done, here." His tone was clipped. Couldn't help it. "I'll stow the wheelbarrow. Just leave your gloves in the tack room and wait for me outside. I'll be right there."

"You're booting me out?"

"No, I... wait for me outside, please."

No answer. Maybe she was ticked. Without checking to see if she was glaring at him, he rolled the wheelbarrow quickly to the rear of the barn and leaned it against the wall. He'd planned to make her dinner and keep his libido in check until after the meal. The pressure behind his fly might not make that plan doable.

"You sound stressed."

He turned and there she was, inches away, her gaze smoldering and her breathing shallow. He swallowed. "It's been a long day."

"It's been a long summer." Tossing the gloves to the floor, she moved in, smoothing her palms up his chest, cupping his face in both hands and pulling him down to meet her full lips.

He ran up the white flag. Grabbing the back of her head, he put his own spin on the kiss, delving into the moist heat of her hungry mouth. She responded with a groan and pressed her body to his.

Flames licked his privates as he thrust his tongue deep. His cock surged to life. Forget dinner. Forget everything but a kiss with the power to burn away every resolution to keep his emotional distance. This was so *right.* Couldn't she see that? Couldn't she feel it?

As passion raged through him, he was oblivious to everything but the perfect connection of his mouth and hers... until his belt loosened. And the top button of his jeans let go.

He put an inch between his lips and hers. "Val..."

"I want to." She eased down the zipper of his fly. "We did this last time, remember?"

"Yes, but—"

"Let me take the edge off."

"I don't need—"

"Oh, but you do." She slid both hands inside his briefs.

And he was lost. When she dropped to her knees, he turned over the reins. She took him without preamble, without coy licks and kisses. Clearly she wanted him to come, and come fast. He obliged, gritting his teeth to keep from yelling and scaring the horses.

When she finished and slowly released him, he was breathing like a freight train and denting his palms with his fingernails. Somehow he remained standing.

She tucked his happy cock back into his briefs, buttoned his jeans and zipped his fly. She even buckled his belt before she rose to her feet and wound her arms around his neck. "How was that?"

Heart pounding, he wrapped her in his arms and pulled her close, tucking her head under his chin so she couldn't see his face. Tender words of gratitude lodged in his throat. Couldn't say them.

Instead he managed a chuckle. "I'd call that a good start."

8

"I wasn't sure what to bring." Val handed Teague her suitcase and picked up two canvas bags on the floor of the passenger side of her truck. "How long does your mom think I've been here?"

"I kept it vague. I'll take those bags, too."

"Okay, thanks." She gave him the bags one at a time so he could sling one over his shoulder. "I have more stuff behind the seat. I may have brought too much."

"I doubt it. The more stuff, the more convincing this will be." He lifted the second bag. "Books?"

"You guessed it. Paperback romances. Figured that would be a nice touch since I doubt you read them."

"Not yet. Maybe I'll start."

She flashed him a grin. "I could read one of the sexy times scenes to you. Put you in the mood."

"That won't be a problem, but I like the idea." He stood patiently holding a large suitcase and two heavy bags as if they weighed nothing. Quite the manly performance.

"Why don't you take those in? I'll be right behind you."

"No worries. I'll wait while you grab the rest. Can you get it okay?"

"Absolutely." She knew better than to insist. He was a cowboy, and although he'd promised not to get mushy, he'd need a brain transplant to get rid of his gentlemanly manners. She flipped the front seat forward and lifted two more bags from the backseat. "All set."

"After you."

She lugged the bags up the porch steps and set one down so she could open the screen door.

"Just leave it open for now."

"Will do." She walked into his tidy living room. Would he have flowers waiting? The old Teague would have. Nope. No flowers. But the room looked different. "Did you move the furniture around?"

"Yes, ma'am."

"The couch used to be in front of the fireplace." Now it was perpendicular to the hearth, with both easy chairs across from it and the coffee table in the middle.

"I decided it looked better this way."

"Very nice." And less convenient for making out in front of the fireplace. "When did you change it?"

"Not really sure. A while ago."

Likely the day after she'd rejected his proposal. "Should I just take these back to the bedroom?"

"If that's where they go."

"More or less. Bedroom and bathroom."

"I cleared a shelf for you in the bathroom and made room in the shower."

"Thanks." She took the all-too-familiar walk back to his bedroom. "This feels weird."

"Déjà vu?"

"Not really. Before I was only here for the weekend. Now I'm moving in, or pretending to. I've never lived with a guy."

"No?" He sounded surprised.

"Like I said back in June, I value my independence. Once I was out of college and could afford a place of my own, I jumped at the chance to have complete privacy."

"So if I'd asked you to move in instead of proposing, you would have refused that, too?"

"Yep. But... that would have been an easier conversation." She stepped through the door of his bedroom and set her bags on the polished wood floor. No sheets turned back or mints on the pillow. "This looks different, too." She'd been too focused on him the previous night to notice.

"I like the bed pushed against the far wall. You catch the breeze from the window."

"You got a new comforter." Light gray instead of dark brown.

"A store in Great Falls had a sale."

She'd hurt him more than he'd ever let on. The evidence was all around her — a rearranged living room and bedroom, new linens on the bed. His sheets and comforter had been in great shape. Most guys didn't switch those things out because they were tired of the color. "Did you buy new towels, too?"

"It was an awesome sale."

She turned back to him. "The walls weren't yellow before, either."

"They were a little dinged up." He avoided her gaze.

Dinged up. No doubt from the many times their wild lovemaking had slammed the headboard against the wall. Staring at those scuff marks wouldn't have been much fun.

"I figured if I had to paint, I might as well change the color while I was at it." He set down the suitcase and both bags. "Why don't I start dinner while you settle in? I left you space in the closet and the top two dresser drawers are empty."

"Thank you."

"I'm the one who should be thanking you." He nudged back his hat. "I didn't realize the concept of living with me was such a scary deal."

"I can handle it for five days."

"That's good." His frown came and went in the blink of an eye. "When I saw all this stuff, I wondered if—"

"Like you said, the more the better if we're trying to convince your mom I live here. I threw in everything but the kitchen sink." She pointed to one of her bags. "I even brought Florence."

"You have a pet?"

"A plant. A pothos."

"I have no idea what that is."

"Exactly. Most bachelors don't have house plants. Most single women have at least one. Florence is mine and having her in the living room will be another signal to your mother that I've moved in."

"She's in that bag?"

"Don't worry. I protected her so she wouldn't get smooshed."

"Better let me take her into the living room, though." He started forward.

"She's fine. She's tough." Her heart stuttered as he kept coming.

"I'm sure she is. But I'm also sure she'd be happier when she can breathe."

That makes two of us. Until this moment, she'd been distracted by the changes he'd made to his surroundings. While she'd processed those, the sensual pull of his body hadn't been an issue. The scent of his aftershave hadn't reached her from across the room.

But now he was close, very close. Crouching down to lift Florence out of the bag, she was eye-level with the fly of his jeans. Her core clenched, dampening her panties. Hands shaking, she freed the plant from its nest and stood on unsteady legs. "Don't give her any water. She doesn't need it."

"Ever?" He took the pot from her, his hands brushing hers during the exchange.

That brief touch set off a tingle that traveled to very erotic locations. "Oh, no, she needs it. Just not right now."

"How about you?" His voice was as smooth as a shot of top-shelf whiskey. "Anything you need right now?"

She couldn't help it. Had to look at him. Big mistake. His knowing glance said he was onto her. Time to regain the upper hand. "I'm hungry, cowboy, *very* hungry."

His eyes darkened. "I can fix that."

"I'm hungry for food."

"Oh." He gave her a sexy grin. "I can fix that, too. I'll holler when dinner's ready." He left, taking Florence with him.

She stood in the middle of his bedroom, confused as hell. Three months ago he would have maneuvered her into bed. She would have gone willingly. Despite what she'd said, she wasn't *that* hungry.

But times had changed. He'd taken her at her word and walked out of the room smiling, the rat. She wanted him to come back and seduce her. But she'd be damned if she'd say so.

9

Florence was a pretty little thing — large, lush leaves, mostly dark green but with some variation in the color on a few of them. He was no expert, but Florence looked young, like she'd barely started her life with Val.

Yet Val had named her and brought her along today. Adorable quirks like that had been part of the reason he'd fallen head over heels back in June. Since he'd never fully recovered from that fall, he'd probably go down in flames sometime in the next five days. Until then, he'd live for the moment.

He put the ceramic blue pot in the middle of the coffee table after checking to make sure there was no drainage hole that would leak water on the handmade coffee table Ed had given him. Florence lived in a smaller plastic flowerpot inside the ceramic one, so no danger of leakage.

Hanging his hat on a hook by the door, he headed for the kitchen and washed up. He'd agonized over what to serve Val for dinner. Steak might say he was trying too hard. Hamburgers might say he wasn't trying hard enough.

He'd gone with spaghetti and his homemade sauce. Or rather, his mom's recipe for homemade sauce. He'd made the sauce yesterday and the salad right before leaving for the barn.

A foolproof dinner.

Except his attention wasn't on the task. Instead he wandered to the kitchen door, captured by the rhythmic click as she hung up her clothes, the scrape of wood as she opened dresser drawers, the swish of the shower curtain when she put her shampoo and conditioner on the shelf inside.

He was new at this, too. He'd never moved in with a girlfriend or invited one to move in with him. Val was the first woman he'd asked to share his space. While she'd shrunk from the concept, he'd welcomed it with open arms.

A gurgling sound made him spin toward the stove, where bubbling sauce dotted the stovetop with red splotches and the rolling boil of the pasta guaranteed it would be overcooked. Hell.

While he was in the middle of cleaning spaghetti sauce off the stovetop, she walked into the kitchen. "Oh, my goodness, what happened?"

"A spaceship landed in front of the house and I had to go welcome them to the planet."

"Well, of course you did!" She laughed. "Are they staying for dinner?"

"I asked, but they're allergic to tomato sauce, so they headed over to the Apple Barrel for pie and coffee." He wiped up the final bit of red glop and rinsed the dishcloth under the faucet. "All settled in?"

"Sure am. Spaghetti?"

"That was the idea. I overcooked the noodles while I was chatting with the aliens, so I'll need to make another batch. Won't take long."

"Don't bother. I don't care if the spaghetti's mushy."

"I do." He dumped out the noodles and ran fresh water in the pot. She didn't want mushy speeches and she wouldn't get mushy noodles, either.

"Have it your way, then. What are we drinking?"

"Ed insisted I serve champagne." He turned the burner on high and took the package of noodles out of the cupboard. "It's chilling in the fridge. You're welcome to open it if you—"

"No, sir, I'm leaving that to you. I need more practice on the cheap kind before I tackle a bottle from Ed's stash."

"I'll do it after I get the noodles going. Glasses are in the—"

"Top cupboard on the end. I remember." She crossed to the cabinet and opened the door. "Wow, I don't remember you having honest-to-goodness champagne glasses before."

"Just got 'em from Ed. She called them an engagement present."

"Hold on." She turned, a crystal flute in each hand. "You're making me nervous. Please tell me Ed understands that—"

"She was kidding." He added the noodles to the boiling water, turned down the heat and checked the time. He'd used the last ones in the box, so he couldn't afford to screw it up again.

"I hope she was kidding."

"I can guarantee it. She wasn't happy with the way I handled things in June." Fetching the bottle of champagne from the fridge, he peeled off the foil.

"I wondered about that." She set the flutes on the kitchen counter. "I thought about contacting her to see if we were still friends. But I was afraid she might blame me for what happened so I chickened out."

"Put your mind at rest. She totally blames me." He started untwisting the wire on the neck of the bottle.

"Wait." She stepped closer. "I want to watch how you do this. The last time Nell and I shared a bottle, we made a mess."

"Sometimes that's the point." He loosened the cage but left it in place.

"To make it go everywhere? What a waste of good champagne."

"I probably wouldn't do it with Ed's, but if you're opening grocery store champagne, it's fun to let the cork shoot out. There's even a technique called sabering where you knock the neck off the bottle and it erupts like Old Faithful."

"That sounds like a guy thing."

"It could be a girl thing, too."

"I suppose, but I'll bet women would rather drink it than let it shoot out the neck of the bottle." She smirked at him.

Oh. "I... um... hadn't thought of it that way." His cock stirred.

"How could you not? It's clearly a male fantasy, the perfect stand-in for—"

"Never mind." He tightened his grip on the cork and clenched his jaw.

"You look flustered."

"It's just that this is the critical part, and the cork is trying to push its way out of the bottle."

"Do tell."

"Val, cut it out or it really will go everywhere."

She started laughing. "You're not in control of it?"

"So far I am, but—"

"Poor baby. I'll shut up. Please proceed with taking the wire off."

"If you don't want an explosion, you leave the wire on. It helps hold the cork in check."

"Aha. That's where Nell and I went wrong. We thought if we wanted what was inside that bottle, we had to strip off everything."

His jeans began to pinch. "You do realize you're torturing me."

"Sorry. Torture for you, but fun for me."

"I can tell. Are you watching?"

"Like a hawk."

"Are you right-handed?"

"You don't know?"

"I think you are, but I haven't paid that much attention to whether you're—"

"See how little we know about each other?"

"Val."

"I'm right-handed."

"Good. So am I. Use your right hand to hold the cork and the neck of the bottle."

"Come to think of it, that's how I—"

"Don't you *dare* say it."

She grinned. "Okay, go on."

He cleared his throat. "Grip the bottom with your left. Twist the bottle one way and the cork the other. Like this." The cork eased out with a soft sigh. "No eruption."

"Now I'm kind of sad that the poor bottle didn't get to—"

"That does it." He rammed the cork back in and put the champagne in the fridge. Flipping the knobs on the stove, he turned off the burners and grabbed her hand. "I'm taking you to bed."

_10_

Val got the giggles as Teague, a man on a mission, pulled her through the living room and down the hall. "What about the spaghetti? Won't that batch be ruined, too?"

"To hell with the spaghetti." He lengthened his stride. "We'll worry about it after we attend to a few things."

"Sounds serious."

"Damned straight." He barreled through the doorway and pulled her close. "You messed with the wrong guy, lady."

She gazed into eyes glittering with frustrated passion. "What about the champagne?"

"It'll keep. This won't." His mouth came down on hers, his tongue demanding entrance as he began working her out of her clothes.

She followed his lead, unbuckling his belt, unfastening the button of his jeans. They'd perfected this routine three months ago and they hadn't lost a step. Breathing hard, they tumbled to his king-sized bed and rolled into position.

Teague threaded his fingers through hers, pressed her hands to the mattress and leaned down to delve into her mouth once again. Lowering his lightly furred chest, he brushed lazily over her taut nipples, creating a friction designed to drive her insane. The thrust of his tongue grew more suggestive as he mimicked the very action she yearned for. Moisture dampened her thighs.

She was writhing against the comforter by the time he lifted his head to gaze down at her. "You're a terrible tease, Valerie Jenson."

She gulped for air. "It takes one to know one."

"I should make you wait for it."

"Betcha can't." She dragged in a breath. "Not when you know how good it will feel." Her skin flushed in anticipation. "Not when you remember what it's like when the cork comes out of the bottle."

"I can hold out a while longer." He sounded mellow, but the intensity in his eyes gave the lie to that boast. "You took the edge off, remember?"

"Not much, judging from your reaction in the kitchen." She ran her tongue slowly over her lips.

A muscle twitched in his jaw. "I held it together."

"Barely."

"I'm in control of my urges." He tightened his grip on her hands. "And in control of you."

"That's what you think." She stroked his muscled calf with her foot, rubbing slowly back and forth.

"Doesn't bother me."

"Then why are you breathing faster?"

"You just think I am." He pressed down gently with his chest. "See? Perfectly calm."

"Your heart's beating really fast." She arched her back, pushing against him, craving contact. "You're ready to explode."

He swallowed. "Am not."

"You should get the condom you tucked under the pillow before it's too late."

"Found that, did you?"

"I know all your tricks."

"So you think."

"Let me put it on for you. Remember that sensation when you sink into my—"

"You win." Releasing her right hand, he reached under the pillow and pulled out the foil package. "I'd better do this, though."

"Let me do it." She plucked the condom from his fingers. "It's not like it's hard."

His smile was strained. "I beg to differ."

"Now who's talking dirty?" She ripped open the package.

"You started it."

"Good thing I did. I thought we'd never get in here." She tossed the wrapper aside.

"You're the one who wanted food. I was being civilized."

"Forget that noise."

"I... ahhh." He closed his eyes as she rolled the condom on. "Your hands on me... feel... way too good."

"Still in complete control?" She circled his girth with her fingers and squeezed gently. "See, I do use my right hand."

"Don't care, don't care, don't care."

"It's cork popping time?"

"Not if I can help it." He pried her fingers loose. "I have a lot to accomplish before that happens." Braced on one arm, he guided his cock to her entrance.

Her heart thundered. "Like what?"

"Like turning you inside out." He pushed deep.

She moaned, reveling in the pleasure of their perfect connection.

"I take it you like that?"

"You know I do."

"Then let's get this done." Dipping his head, he nibbled on her earlobe, his breath warm as he eased out and drove in again. His voice dropped to a sexy murmur. "And I promise it won't be the least bit civilized." He nipped her ear.

Her yelp of surprise was cut short as he slipped his hands under her hips, lifting her as he rose to his knees.

Feet in the air, hands clutching the comforter, she abandoned herself to an erotic position in which he had all the control and she had none. Turned out that cowboy knew what he was doing. In no time, she was yelling his name as her first climax arrived, followed quickly by another.

He maintained the tight connection, his cock buried securely in her quivering channel as he lowered her, gasping and limp, back to the mattress. He moved over her and placed a kiss on her damp forehead. "Did I do it?"

She took a ragged breath. "Do what?"

"Turn you inside out." He touched his lips to her eyelids.

"Uh-huh."

"You're sure?"

"Very sure." She let out a happy sigh. "I'm so inside out I don't want to move. Ever."

"Then don't. Pretend I'm not here." He pumped slowly, gliding easily on the liquid path he'd created.

"That's lovely." She opened her eyes and gazed into his. "But is it enough?"

"Enough?"

"To push the cork out of the bottle."

Amusement flashed in his eyes. "Yes, ma'am. I could come now, but I don't want to."

"Why not?"

"I'd rather bring you along with me."

"Dream on. We never made it to three before."

He continued his easy pace. "Doesn't mean it couldn't happen."

"I don't have the energy."

"That's fine. Just lie still." He shifted his position slightly.

"That's my plan. I... what did you just do?"

"Nothing."

"Yes, you did. You changed your angle." A ripple of awareness traveled through her core.

"Not much."

"That was sneaky."

He grinned. "Don't you dare move."

"You're not the boss of me." She cupped his glutes and rose to meet his next stroke. "Mm. Not bad."

"Maybe even good?"

"Maybe. You can go faster if you want."

"If you insist." He stepped it up. In seconds his breathing changed and his eyes darkened.

Clearly he was getting close. His arousal fueled hers and she dug her fingers into his flexing muscles, urging him to go deeper.

With a groan, he opened the throttle. His rapid thrusts brought her to the brink and hurled her over. The rush of his orgasm blended with hers, inspiring a jubilant *woo-hoo!*

His answering shout of *yeah, baby!* made her laugh, which added a whole new dimension to the sensations dancing through her quivering body. What a party. And it was just beginning.

_11_

So far, so good. Teague had made energetic and highly emotional love to Val without uttering a single endearment. Maybe he was getting the hang of this.

He didn't linger in bed, though. Taking care of the condom provided the perfect excuse to get the hell out of there before he said something he shouldn't.

When he walked back into the bedroom, she had her back to him as she smoothed the wrinkles out of the comforter. She'd put on a red cotton sleep shirt that reached to mid-thigh. "Hi, there."

"If you're straightening up, we must be done."

"For now." Giving the comforter one more swipe with her palm, she turned to face him.

The slogan on the front of her shirt made him smile. _You can't scare me. I teach 4th grade._ "I see you brought nightwear."

"I thought I should since you don't always remember to close the curtains and your mother will be within walking distance of this house."

"She won't show up unannounced."

"I'm not taking any chances. Do you own pajamas?"

He made a face.

"Oh, now I remember. You're a sweats and T-shirt guy."

"That I am, and since we're dressing for dinner, I'll put something on." He crossed to the bureau and automatically opened the top drawer. Sexy panties and bras in neat piles had replaced his folded T-shirts and briefs.

"You're welcome to anything in there." Laughter rippled in her voice.

"Not my jam." He closed the drawer and opened the third one down.

"Don't knock it until you've tried it. I've heard of guys getting turned on by wearing—"

"That's the last thing I need." He'd had to combine the contents of two drawers into one. He extracted a smooshed shirt and a tightly rolled pair of sweats. "Especially after a certain someone makes opening a champagne bottle an erotic episode."

"I simply pointed out the obvious. And it's not just champagne that gets phallic treatment. Boys love shaking a bottle of pop and letting it spew out."

"I'll bet girls do, too." He pulled on his sweats and tied the drawstring.

"Do they really? When was the last time you saw that?"

"Just because I haven't seen it doesn't mean it doesn't happen." He shook the wrinkles from his shirt.

"But it's rare. On the other hand, when a camera crew films a locker room after a football team wins a championship, you'll always see bottles of stuff spraying everywhere."

"Well, sure. It's a fun way to celebrate." He shoved his arms into the sleeves of his shirt and popped it over his head, tugging it down over his chest. When he looked up, Val was staring at him. "What?"

"It is a fun way to celebrate." Her gaze warmed. "Maybe shaking a bottle and spraying the contents is what you do when you don't have the option of wonderful sex."

Maybe he'd played it a little too cool. "It was great, Val."

"It felt like a celebration."

Yes. His brain stalled. Was *she* getting mushy? If she did, he'd fold like a deck of cards. Dangerous territory, here. He took a quick breath and gave her a big effing smile. "It sure did." He almost added *by golly* for good measure.

There. He'd just downplayed a transcendent sexual experience with the woman he loved by treating it like a sports victory. Would she buy it?

"Three times. I still can't believe it."

Hm. What they'd shared might be like a sports victory to her if she was keeping score. "Now we know you can."

"It might've been a fluke."

"I guess we'll find out." He wanted to be done with the topic. His goal had been to have her come when he did, to be lost in the glory of it together, their bodies completely in tune. She might have missed all that. And he needed to let it go. "What do you say we order a pizza?"

"Do you have any of that canned chili we ate last time?"

"Yes, ma'am, but we only ate that because we didn't want to waste time cooking and ordering a pizza meant putting on clothes to answer the door."

"You just made my case for me."

"Canned chili and champagne?"

"Why not? Were you planning to have a salad to go with the spaghetti?"

"Already put together. It's in the fridge."

"Crackers for the chili?"

"I have some."

"Sounds like a meal. C'mon." She tilted her head toward the doorway. "I'll heat up the chili while you organize everything else."

"You've got a deal." He followed her out of the bedroom.

They'd had many such moments during their weekend together in June — cozy and domestic exchanges after enjoying a terrific time in the sack. No wonder he'd proposed after only a week.

His steps slowed. Damn, she'd been right about this setup. She'd warned him that living as an engaged couple would put him right back in marriage mode. He'd been convinced it wouldn't. But he was already there.

"Teague? Are you coming?"

He snapped out of his daze and strolled into the kitchen, a cool dude with nothing but sex on his mind. "Been there, done that."

"Very funny." She had two cans of chili, one in each hand. "Feels like a two-can night."

"It does."

"Remind me where you keep the can opener."

"In that drawer." He pointed to it.

"Oh, right!" She flashed him a grin before turning around and fetching the opener. "You prefer a hand job."

"And here we go." He rolled his eyes because she expected him to. "I can't wait for you to say things like that in front of my mother." True statement.

"I won't. I just do it with you because I get such a great reaction."

"You don't have to censor yourself unless the girls are around." He crossed to the refrigerator and took out the salad and the champagne. "If it's all adults, my mom would get a kick out of your zingers."

"You know, that's what I'm afraid of." She opened the cans and rummaged in the cupboard for a large saucepan.

"Why?"

"What if your mom and I like each other?" She set her chosen pan on the stove, dumped in the chili and turned on the burner.

"I think you will. Seems like a plus." He grabbed a bottle of dressing. He could make his own, but after the tip from Riley and Claire, he'd toned down his urge to over-deliver.

"You'd think it would be a plus, wouldn't you? But I'll like it better if we don't get along. I won't feel so guilty about lying to her." She took a wooden spoon out of a crock on the stove and stirred the chili.

He blew out a breath. "Gotcha. I have guilt pangs, too."

"What if you leveled with her once she gets here?"

"I can't risk it." He got out both salad and soup bowls. "All I'd do is confirm her fear that I'll die alone."

"That's ridiculous. You're a great guy and a talented lover. You have your own house and a steady job. You won't end up alone."

"Tell that to my mother. I'm thirty-one. She thinks that's—"

"Well, thirty-one *is* old, now that you mention it." She tapped the spoon on the side of the pan and laid it in the spoon holder. "It's a miracle you can still perform in the bedroom."

"And how old are you, smartass?"

"I'm just a kid of twenty-nine."

"A babe in the woods." He uncorked the champagne and filled both glasses. "It's a wonder you put up with an old codger like me."

"I prefer a man with some experience."

He carried the glasses to the stove. "You mean one who knows how to open a champagne bottle?" He handed over one of the flutes.

"Well, yes, and..." Heat flickered in her eyes. "I was impressed with that nifty position you used. You've never—"

"I was saving it for a special occasion." He met her gaze and lifted his glass. "To nifty positions."

"And the thrills they create." She tapped her flute against his and sipped. "Damn, this is good stuff."

He swallowed, the fizz dancing on his tongue. "Glad you like it. Ed gave me several bottles."

"Several? What's she up to?"

"With Ed, I wouldn't dare to guess."

"I would. She likes me and would love to see us become a couple. She figures champagne won't hurt and might help."

"That sounds about right." He took another sip. "I told her how it is."

"Thanks." She studied him over the rim of her glass, frowning in concentration.

"I feel like a bug under a microscope."

She blinked. "Sorry. It's just that I can't figure out why you're still single."

"Neither can my mom."

"You'd make someone a terrific husband. Apple Grove's small, but not that small. What's the stumbling block?"

He shrugged. "Turns out I'm extremely picky."

"You should be if you're choosing the person you'll be with the rest of your life. Have you had any close calls, at least?"

"Besides you?"

"Obviously besides me. I can't believe I'm the only woman who's caught your eye in all the years you've lived here."

"Well, there was Millie."

"Jake's Millie?"

"Yes, ma'am. Everybody, me included, assumed she was Jake's girl. Then it looked like she'd given up on him, so I moved in. That was just what Jake needed to lay his claim. I was SOL."

"I can't imagine you with Millie."

"Why not?"

"It's hard to explain. She's feisty, and you need someone like that, but... I don't know. You two don't quite fit."

"Obviously, since she married Jake." Was Val a little jealous? She acted like it. Might be wishful thinking on his part, though.

"I had this fantasy that if all goes well in the next few days, we could keep dating after your mom leaves."

His chest tightened. "What a coincidence. I have that same fantasy. I wouldn't ask you to move in. I realize that's not appealing to you, but maybe you'd be willing to spend the weekend out here sometimes."

"That would be nice."

"Great! I'm glad you—"

"And extremely selfish."

"What?"

"How do you expect to find a wife if I'm monopolizing your free time?"

"Let me worry about that."

"But will you? My guess is you'll abandon the search and just have fun dating me."

"Nothing wrong with that."

"There is if you were telling me the truth when you proposed."

He winced. He'd laid his soul bare that night as he struggled to convince her they were meant for each other. Instead, every heartfelt word had driven another nail into his coffin.

"If you want a family as much as you said you do, then you need to work harder to make that happen."

"And I will... eventually."

"Eventually isn't going to cut it. Women eager for that life are looking for men like you. Who knows how many good prospects will marry someone else while you're wasting time with me?"

Her logic was flawless. He had no comeback, so he took another gulp of champagne.

"I can tell you don't want to hear this, but hanging out with me will keep you from reaching your goals."

He sighed. "You sound like a teacher."

"Funny thing about that." Her voice softened. "I care about you, which means I need to get out of your way."

He panicked. "Not yet, please. If my mom arrives to find me no longer engaged, she'll—"

"Right, right. I'm talking about what needs to happen after she leaves."

"You're depressing the hell out of me."

"Look, it won't be like it was back in June. We'll part friends. No bad feelings, just an understanding that we want different things."

"So this is our last hurrah?"

She smiled. "Something like that."

"Then let's make the most of it."

<u>12</u>

Oh, what a night. And oh, how quickly dawn arrived. Val woke to the faint hiss of the shower and the aroma of coffee. A strip of light showed under the closed bathroom door. Teague was likely hoping to slip out and handle the barn chores by himself. Not happening.

Throwing back the covers, she climbed out of bed and stretched. He'd made a playground of her body during the night and she'd returned the favor. They'd tried to sleep, but three months of abstinence had created a powerful hunger. Exhaustion hadn't claimed them until the wee hours.

She quickly made the bed. When the shower shut off, she walked over and tapped on the bathroom door. "My turn."

He opened it, a towel draped around his hips and drops of water clinging to his chest hair. She wanted to lick them off.

"I was trying to be quiet."

"That's very sweet of you, but I want to help feed and I—"

"Hang on, I have to do this." He cupped the back of her head and kissed her with infinite tenderness. Then he lifted his head. "Good morning."

Her heart melted. "Good morning to you, too."

"Can I talk you into going back to bed?"

"With you?"

"Alone, I'm afraid."

"Then I'm staying up. I've been looking forward to barn chores. All I need is a shower and a cup of that coffee. I'll be right as rain."

He opened the door wider and motioned her in. "It's all yours. If you can make do with coffee for now, we'll come back and eat breakfast after we're done."

"Thanks. I keep meaning to compliment the concierge on the service in this place." She moved past him into the steamy bathroom.

He smiled. "You had a satisfying evening?"

"Very satisfying." She looked him up and down. "Something's moving under your towel."

"Ah, you know how it is with this guy. Give him an inch and he'll take a mile."

"I like that about him."

His eyes darkened. Reaching for her, he drew her close. His nostrils flared. "You smell delicious."

"I smell like sex."

"Exactly."

"I need a shower."

His voice dropped to a seductive murmur. "I'd rather give you a tongue bath."

Her breath caught as her core tightened. One suggestive comment was all it took. "But we have to—"

"Yes, ma'am." Regret in his gaze, he released her. "Better go take your shower. And close the door."

"Should I lock it?"

"Do I sound that deranged?"

"Maybe."

His glance swept over her, lingering on her tight nipples before sliding down to her trembling thighs. With a soft groan, he turned away. "Lock it."

Heart thundering, she closed the door softly and twisted the lock. Three months ago they'd been eager lovers, but nothing compared to this. The ticking clock could be why.

Would she let him postpone his duties for another round? If he dressed and left the bedroom while she was in the shower, she wouldn't have to test her resolve. If she came out to find him lying in bed waiting for her....

He wasn't. The clink of plates and glasses told her he was unloading the dishwasher.

After pulling on underwear and a pair of cotton socks, she dressed in jeans and an old knit shirt. She'd brought some knockabout clothes specifically for working in the barn.

She'd pinned her hair on top of her head for the shower, so all it needed was a good brushing. She tied it back with a thin leather string he'd given her in June to tame her hair during the riding lessons.

It worked better than her scrunchies so she'd kept using it, even after the breakup. But the significance of a string wasn't lost on her. When this episode was over and she'd sworn off Teague for good, she'd find an alternative hair tie.

She'd been the one to suggest a quick end to this lovely relationship, but starting off the day with that hanging over her head didn't suit her at all. She'd deal with it when the time came. Until then she'd enjoy Teague's good loving. Tugging on her boots, she left the bedroom.

He was pouring coffee into a stoneware mug when she walked into the kitchen.

"Is that for me?"

"As a matter of fact."

"Great timing."

"I heard your boots hit the floor." He handed her the mug and picked up his phone.

"Thanks." She took a sip.

"Ed texted a couple minutes ago. She invited us up to the house for breakfast after we're done, but she said it wasn't obligatory."

"Oh, I think it is." She cradled the mug in both hands as she sipped. Teague made good love and good coffee.

"Trust me, it's not a command performance. Ed and I got everything sorted out on Monday night. If she says we don't have to come, she means it."

"What exactly did you sort out?"

"Where she stands on this deal."

"Are you sure she's not upset with me?"

"Far from it. She's been an independent woman all her life and she recognizes that you're cut from the same cloth. After we broke up, she said my timing was atrocious and you were right to call it quits after I showed such bad judgment."

She flinched. "That must have hurt."

"It did at the time. I've had three months to forgive myself."

A guy who could accept criticism, learn from it and move on. Appealing. "What did she say about me on Monday night?"

"She thinks you're a good friend to help me out and she fully expects us to have a hot time while you're here. If we'd rather go back to bed than have breakfast with her, she won't be offended."

Her cheeks warmed. "She said that?"

"Not in so many words, but it was implied."

"I can't speak for you, but I'm not cheeky enough to decline Ed's breakfast invitation so you and I can get it on."

"I'll tell her we'll be there in about forty-five minutes." He sent the text and glanced at her. "How're you doing on that coffee?"

She polished it off. "Done." She crossed to the dishwasher and put her mug inside. "Let's go." She headed out of the kitchen.

"Did you bring a hat?"

"I left it in the truck. I can grab it on the way. I— hang on. Can't leave yet."

"Why not?"

"I have to water Florence. She's due. It'll just take a sec." She picked up the pot from the coffee table and carried it into the kitchen.

He followed. "Why bring it in here? Why not take a glass of water out there?"

"Because this is better. No danger she'll sit in old water." She lifted the plastic pot into the sink, ran water into it and let it drain. "That will take care of her until I leave, although I check on her every day to make sure she's not too moist or too dry."

She put her back in the ceramic container. "There you go, Florence."

"I've never seen anyone talk to their plants."

"It's good for them. They need the carbon dioxide from our breath. I think she likes it where you put her. Lots of ambient light." She replaced Florence on the coffee table. "Ready."

"Then let's do it." He plucked his hat from a coat tree by the door and ushered her out on the porch. "We should have time to take that ride this morning after we clean the stalls." He closed the door behind them.

"To clarify, you're talking about a horseback ride, right?" She glanced over her shoulder.

"I was." Grasping her arm, he turned her around and pulled her close. "Until you said that. Is there something you'd rather do?"

"Yes, and I'll bet it's the same thing you'd rather do."

"Then let's forget about the horseback ride." He cupped her bottom, kneading with his fingers. "We can ride horses when my mom's here."

"Whatcha got in mind?" She pressed closer, the hard ridge behind his fly a potent reminder of the hours they'd spent pleasuring each other.

"Don't know if you remember, but cleaning stalls is sweaty work."

Her heart raced. "I seem to recall that."

"What else do you remember?"

"Sweaty sex on a bed of straw when we finished."

"Haven't been able to make myself put a horse in that stall since that day."

"Same straw?"

He smiled and shook his head. "I refreshed it."

"When?"

"Yesterday."

"Did you tuck a condom into that little space between the boards like you did before?"

"I might have."

"Why didn't you say so? Why even bring up the horseback ride?"

"Because last night you said that would be nice and for all I know, making love on a bed of straw in the barn wasn't as much fun for you as it was for me."

"It was big fun for me. I'd never done anything like that. The scent of straw turns me on, now."

"It does?"

"That's why I couldn't keep my hands to myself after we were done feeding. And why I made sure I was never alone with you in the barn during the lessons over at the Buckskin. I was afraid I'd tackle you."

He grinned. "I had no idea. Then you're good with this plan?"

"I am."

"Listen, if straw affects you like an aphrodisiac, maybe you should skip the feeding. Either that or we should cancel breakfast with Ed."

"No worries. I'm a lot less frustrated than when I arrived. And I'm way less frustrated than

I've been all summer. I can control myself long enough to deliver a few hay flakes and some oats."

"You're sure?"

"Absolutely. Especially if I have something to look forward to."

13

Straw. A secret he might never have discovered about Val if he hadn't cooked up this fake fiancée caper.

He didn't take her hand as they headed over to the barn in the soft light of dawn. "When my mom arrives, I'll need to hold your hand when we're walking somewhere together."

"Or we could stick our hands in each other's back jeans pocket."

"Let's not."

She chuckled. "That wouldn't work for you?"

"It's too dangerous. No telling how I'd react if you're cupping my ass for any length of time. Or I'm cupping yours, for that matter."

"Okay, no ass-grabbing. What do you think we should call each other?"

"How about Teague and Val?"

"I don't know if just using our plain old names will convince your mom we're engaged. We might need to come up with cutesy nicknames."

"Like what?"

"I could call you the Teague-man."

"No, you couldn't."

"Teague-a-roony?"

He sighed. "Having fun?"

"Yes, I am. I've never been pseudo-engaged before. Might as well make the most of it."

"I think we can skip the cutesy nicknames, if it's all the same to you, Val-a-rini." He slid back the double barn doors.

She laughed. "That's not bad."

"It's terrible. *Valerie* is a beautiful name and *Val* is easy on the tongue, but—"

"Easy on the tongue? Which part of me is the easiest, would you say?"

"All of you, devil woman. All of you." He motioned her inside. "Payback time. Breathe deep. Lots of straw in here."

"I can take it." She marched inside and made for the tack room. "I'll fetch our gloves, unless you have a special pair."

"They're all the same. Just bring two pairs, please." He lengthened his stride, determined to get his hands on the wheelbarrow in the back of the barn before his libido sent him into the tack room so he could get his hands on Val. Now that she'd revealed her vulnerability to the aroma of straw, she was even more tempting.

The last stall on the left held the stash of hay flakes and he directed his energy toward loading the wheelbarrow. Val came toward him with his gloves and his movements slowed. Damn, she was gorgeous.

"How come you didn't wait for me to bring your gloves?" She handed them to him.

"Eager to get started, I guess."

"I see that look in your eye, cowboy. We're not doing what you're thinking about. We're saving it for after we muck out the stalls later. Think about something else."

"Turns out I can't. Remember which stall it was?"

"The one right across from you." She pointed to it. "It's not only straw that affects me. I could smell the hay flakes, too. The combination inspired me to give you that special treat yesterday."

He groaned. "Grab a hay flake, please, before I lose my cool and grab you."

"Sure, okay. I'll start with Sir Eatsalot."

"Good choice."

He worked fast, which meant he'd delivered to everybody on his side before she was done. "I'll get the oats while you finish up."

"In a hurry, cowboy?"

"Yes, ma'am."

Her soft laughter ramped up his tension another notch. She could seduce him without even trying. A look, a sigh, a knowing grin and he was off to the races. No other woman had that effect on him.

By the time he'd passed out oats to those who were scheduled to get them, she'd completed her deliveries. Turning the wheelbarrow around, she rolled it toward the back of the barn. He resisted the impulse to walk in that direction. Sure as the world, he'd kiss her if he got within range.

Then again, she hadn't put on lipstick this morning, had she? One little kiss wasn't such a bad idea. His body hummed with anticipation as he tucked his gloves in his back pocket and started down the aisle.

"I hear your purposeful stride." She leaned the wheelbarrow against the wall, turned around and took off her gloves. "Is there a reason for that?"

"Could be."

Her eyes glittered. "Changed your mind about when we'll have our rendezvous in the stall?"

"No, ma'am. I want to take my time, make the most of the experience. We wouldn't have that luxury if we try to squeeze it in, now."

"You look like you're in the mood to squeeze something, though."

"I am." Nudging back his hat, he stepped forward and slid his hands around her waist. "Since you're not wearing lipstick...."

"Your voice is getting all growly." She dropped her gloves and wound her arms around his neck. "I like it when you sound like that."

"I like it when you let me kiss you." Dipping under the brim of her hat, he indulged himself, thrusting his tongue into her sweet mouth. When she whimpered, he cupped her firm bottom and tucked her in close. Ahh. If only... but not now.

She pressed closer and he tightened his grip. God, she turned him on. Her low moan sent the blood pounding through his veins. Lifting his head, he took a ragged breath. "We have to stop."

"I know."

He let her go and backed away, but that stall looked more tempting by the second. "What if I text Ed? I could tell her that we—"

"Please don't text her. She'd see through any excuse you make and that would embarrass the heck out of me." She met his gaze. "It's just that I've never felt this sensual, this *alive*. I wish we could go away somewhere and just...."

"Make love?"

"Yeah. Isn't that crazy?"

"No." His chest tightened with regret. If he hadn't rushed that proposal, they could have spent the entire summer exploring the possibilities. He'd had a shot. *They'd* had a shot. And he'd blown it. "It's a wonderful idea."

"Impractical, though."

"For now. But—"

"No, it's impractical, full stop." She picked up her gloves. "Might as well leave these here. Want to give me yours?"

"Sure." He pulled them out of his back pocket.

She laid both pairs next to the wheelbarrow. "Ready to go?"

"Yes, ma'am." Heart heavy, he followed her out of the barn.

14

Val climbed the hill to Ed's house walking next to Teague, but not touching him. He'd announced he'd start holding her hand after his mom arrived. She hated to admit that she wanted him to hold her hand now.

What was happening to her? She wasn't the kind of woman who longed to spend days in a secret hideaway with her lover. She cherished her autonomy, took pleasure in being in control of her own space. She'd worried that moving in with Teague would give her claustrophobia.

Instead she wanted more time with the guy, more cuddling, more touching, more Teague. Sexual satisfaction was part of the appeal, but mostly she craved the joy of being close to him, cocooned in the warmth of his arms. She couldn't seem to get enough of that.

"Are you okay?"

"I'm fine. Why?"

"You're just... quiet."

"I was thinking about this hand-holding business."

"What about it?"

"We didn't do much hand-holding in June. I can't remember your preferred style."

"There's a style?"

"At least two I can think of. You can turn your hand sideways and curl your fingers over the back of my hand or you can thread your fingers through my fingers. Which one do you like?"

"Never thought about it. Does it matter?"

"Maybe not, but I'll bet engaged couples choose one or the other and stick to that style. We should look comfortable with the way we're doing it."

He held out his hand. "Let's try the first one."

"Okay." She slipped her hand into his and the knot of tension in her stomach relaxed. "That's nice."

"I like it, too, but we need to test 'em both." Shifting his hand position, he laced his fingers through hers and tightened his grip. "That's better. More secure."

"Way better." Her chest warmed. "The connection is stronger. It's a subtle difference, but—"

"Not that subtle. This is how I held your hands down when I pushed them against the mattress last night. Shoving my fingers in between yours is a form of penetration."

She groaned. "You should *not* have said that."

His soft chuckle added another layer of sensuality. Lifting their clasped hands, he kissed the tips of her fingers. "Don't dish it out if you can't take it."

"But we're almost there. How am I supposed to—"

"I thought I saw you two coming up the path." Ed walked out on the porch wearing purple jeans, a yellow shirt and yellow boots. The jeans, the color of a purple popsicle, matched the streaks in her curly white hair.

"Ed, your hair is fabulous!" Just the distraction she needed right now, too.

"Thanks. My partner-in-crime Ellie Mae Horton drove up from Eagles Nest last month and we spent a wild day at the salon." Her glance lowered to their tightly clasped hands. "Nice touch. You two look extremely engaged."

Teague smiled. "That's the idea."

"Good thing I invited you up here for breakfast. We have things to discuss before Madeline gets here and she'll arrive in less than an hour."

"Less than an *hour*?" Val wished her voice hadn't squeaked on that last word, but losing the chance to make sweaty love on a bed of straw was a blow.

"She must be putting the pedal to the metal." Teague squeezed her hand and released it. "What things do we need to discuss?"

"All the stuff you should know about each other and probably haven't thought to ask."

"You could be right about that." Val climbed the steps, Teague close behind her.

"I'm betting I am. Come on in. I made a list."

Val took her cue from Teague's and left her hat on a coat tree by the door. Then she followed Ed to a sunny dining room that looked out on a walled garden. The climate-controlled space produced blooms, fruit and veggies from April through October. In the evening, lights glittered in the trees and along the pathways. "Your garden looks as amazing as I remember."

"The secret is horse poop. Another reason to keep Sir Eatsalot and Herb. I can't ride them anymore, but they make my garden grow." She waved Val and Teague toward chairs at one end of the sturdy oak table. "Help yourselves to fruit and coffee. The muffins are fresh out of the oven so eat 'em while they're warm. I'll check on our omelets and potatoes." She whisked through an arched doorway into the kitchen.

"Wow." Val surveyed the platters of fruit, a stack of mini donuts and a large basket of muffins. "This is shaping up to be as elaborate as the fancy dinner she served us in June. I only see three plates but it looks like she's expecting more people."

"When we had more hands on the place, she'd put on a big spread for breakfast every morning." He helped her into a chair. "She hasn't quite dialed it back."

"The hands ate at this table?"

"Every meal. Wranglers came from all over to apply for a job. She treated us like family, celebrated our birthdays and included us when she threw her big parties."

"Ed's right about unasked questions. I have no clue how you ended up working here."

"Just like I don't know why you chose to teach here."

"That's easy. I wanted a small school in cowboy country."

"And I thought you were attracted to my sparkling personality."

"That didn't hurt, but the hat, the boots and the jeans got you in the door."

He grinned. "How about what's in the jeans?"

"That's not so bad, either." She sighed. "I guess our stall date is cancelled."

"Afraid so. Maybe we can—"

"Omelets and country fries, anyone?" Ed came in carrying two plates and balancing a third on her arm.

Teague leaped up. "Let me help with that." He relieved her of two plates and set one in front of Val and the other at his place.

"Thanks for the assist." She put down the third plate and smiled at Teague as he held her chair. "I decided to serve you myself so my lovely chef won't be late for her nail appointment. Helps me keep my waitressing skills sharp."

Teague resumed his seat. "Gonna put in an application at the Moose?"

"Wouldn't that be a hoot? Do you think Ben would hire me?"

Val laughed. "He'd be crazy not to."

"I should. It would be a great way to meet men." She glanced at the table. "I see you two haven't managed to eat or drink a single thing while I've been gone. Teague, I'd appreciate it if you'd pour me some coffee." She passed over her mug.

"Yes, ma'am." He picked up the carafe and filled her mug, Val's and his own.

Ed put her napkin in her lap. "Have some of those cherries, Valerie. They're incredible. So are the muffins. I like blueberry, but I feel obliged to serve spiced apple ones, too. Dig in, both of you. You'll need your strength."

Val managed not to spew her coffee. She dabbed at her mouth with a napkin. "Why will I need my strength?"

"To keep up with Madeline. She's a force of nature."

Teague laughed, a forkful of omelet halfway to his mouth. "Like you're not?"

"I have my moments, but she has twenty-five years on me. You should've seen me at her age."

"Wish I had. I'm picturing a force of nature on steroids." He popped the bite of omelet into his mouth.

"I was." Mischief flashed in her eyes, making her look years younger. Then she cleared her throat and picked up a notepad beside her plate. "But we're not here to discuss my past exploits." She consulted her list. "We'll start with the most obvious. How you both ended up in Apple Grove."

Val forked up a bite of country fries. "I've covered my part of that, but I don't know why he's here."

"I claim all the credit. I was competing in a barrel racing event in Eugene and this handsome guy had volunteered to help out during the competition. I asked him to come work for me."

"And everyone said I'd be a fool if I didn't take her up on it."

"Luckily, he wasn't a fool." She gazed at him and sighed. "Not in that case, anyway."

He shrugged. "Pobody's nerfect."

Val laughed. "What?"

"It's a sign on Ed's desk. The first letter of each word—"

"Ah, I get it. Cute."

"And heartbreakingly true." Ed studied her list and glanced at Teague. "Have you told her about your father? That's critical."

"He hasn't." Val took another muffin from the basket and glanced at him. "I was afraid to ask after Jake and Zeke's dad turned out to be so rotten."

"Judging from what my mom says, my dad was the opposite of rotten. He died when I was three, so I don't remember him very well. But she adored that man. Couldn't find anyone half as good, or so she said."

He'd grown up without a dad. Would have been nice to know. "Was it tough for you, not having a father around?"

"I didn't suffer that much. My Uncle Steve, mom's brother-in-law, stepped in. Mom and I spent plenty of time with Uncle Steve, Aunt Julie and my cousins. The family raises horses, so that's how I got into this line of work."

Ed made a checkmark on her list and turned to Val. "What about your parents? Have you told Teague anything about them?"

"There's not much to tell. They live in Lincoln, Nebraska. They're nice people, responsible, hard-working. They took good care of my sister and me."

"Admirable traits." Ed hesitated. "I don't know how to ask this without sounding nosy, but how do they feel about each other?"

"Good, I suppose. They don't fight and they've been married for thirty-three years, so they must..." She met Ed's kind gaze. "They don't spend much time together." She took a quick breath. "I've never said this to anyone, but I think they might be happier living separate lives."

"It happens." Ed patted Val's shoulder. "Sometimes people just grow apart. Nobody's fault. Madeline will ask about Teague's future in-laws, but you can keep the info general. No need to go into depth."

"Good advice. Thanks."

"She's wanted a daughter-in-law for a long time. She'll be full of questions."

Teague nodded. "Yes, she will."

"You know what? I have a question. Why is she so eager for you to get married?"

"A couple of reasons." He put down his coffee mug. "For one thing, she loved being married to my dad and she pictures the same for me, only it'll be better. Chances are I won't lose my spouse at an early age."

"She'll get some vicarious enjoyment from your happiness."

"Right. She also knows I look forward to having a family and she worries that I'm lonely."

"She does worry." Ed pushed her plate aside. "Frankly, I think about it, too. If I hadn't downsized, we'd have more wranglers living here."

"You kept me on, though. That's a huge compliment."

"But it doesn't address the issue. You need company other than me and the horses. But, unlike Madeline, I'm not in a hurry to see you tie the knot."

Val blinked. "Oh?"

"Thirty-one looks damned young from where I sit. There's still plenty of time to make that commitment."

"But Teague wants a family." The words were out of her mouth before she could censor them. "He just said so. Shouldn't he be with someone who—"

"I think he should be with someone whose company he enjoys." She smiled at Teague. "Agreed?"

"I couldn't agree more."

"That's why I'm going along with this fake engagement. I've been itching to tackle this obsession of hers, for her sake and Teague's. This brings the subject to a head. But I digress." She picked up her notepad. "We'll never get through these, so I need to cherry pick. Here's a critical one. If you don't know it, Madeline will cry foul immediately. Can you guess?"

Val looked at Teague. "Favorite ice cream."

"Chocolate. Yours?"

"Coffee."

"That's not it, folks. Guess again."

"Favorite music," Teague said. "I'm country all the way." He turned to Val, eyebrows raised.

"I used to be classical but now I'm country, too."

Their hostess shook her head. "Those are nice add-ons, but not the one I'm thinking of. Give up?"

Teague glanced at his phone. "Time's short. You'd better tell us."

"I'll bet my shelves full of trophies that you don't know each other's middle name."

Val stared at Teague. "I don't know yours."

"'I don't know yours, either. You first."

"Rose."

His eyes widened. "You're kidding."

"It's my grandmother's middle name. I like it, but it's not really me, so I hardly ever—"

"It's my mother's middle name."

She sucked in a breath. "That's freaky. What are the chances?"

"Very good, actually." Ed looked amused. "If you kept up with the tabloids like I do, you'd know that a bunch of Hollywood folks recently used Rose as a middle name for their daughters. Years ago, Sylvester Stallone gave all three of his daughters the middle name of Rose, but that's Sly for you. Marches to a different drummer."

"So maybe it's not so freaky." What a relief. She was already off-balance. A rare coincidence would tip her world sideways. "What's your middle name, Teague-a-roony?"

Ed snorted. "You call him that?"

"I suggested it when we discussed cutsie names. He didn't care for it."

"Gee, I wonder why."

"It sounds like a packaged pasta mix. Anyway, my middle name is Wesley. It was my dad's name."

"Teague Wesley Sullivan." She studied him. "It suits you. I like it."

"I like yours, too, Valerie Rose Jenson." He flashed her a smile. "You might not like Valerie Rose but I think it's pretty."

"I don't hate it." She hated it even less coming out of his mouth. He gave the name a certain something.

"I think that's enough for now." Ed pushed back her chair. "You two should take off, get those ponies turned out and muck the stalls before Madeline gets here."

Teague stood. "We'll help you clean up before we leave."

"Thanks, but not necessary."

He picked up his plate. "We can at least clear the table."

"Absolutely." Val followed his lead and put her silverware on her plate as she pushed back her chair.

"Nope, nope." Ed left her seat and shooed them away. "I want that barn spic and span when she arrives. She always comments on it and I don't want her to think my standards are slipping."

"Yes, ma'am." He gave her a smile. "You're the boss."

"Damn right. I'll text you when she arrives."

Val put down her plate. "Thank you for this wonderful breakfast and for making that list."

"You're so welcome. It gave me a chance to get to know you better, too." Her clear-eyed gaze held nothing back. "I like you, Valerie. Whatever happens, don't be a stranger."

"I won't. I promise." The offer of friendship tugged at her heart. "I like you, too."

15

Teague reached for Val's hand as they walked back down the hill to the barn and slid his fingers through hers.

She glanced over at him, her eyes shadowed by her hat. "Practicing?"

"Thought I'd better. It's almost show time." And he'd use any excuse to touch her.

"Do you think your mom will believe we're engaged?"

"She'll want to, especially after she's spent five minutes with you. You're her type, just like you're Ed's type." *And mine.*

"I do feel a connection to Ed. She's a very wise lady. She's the first person who's asked that about my parents and it was a relief to finally put it into words."

"You never talked about it with your sister?"

"She's so mired in her own problems I didn't want to bring it up."

"No wonder you think of marriage as a trap."

She met his comment with silence.

"Guess I shouldn't have said that."

"It's okay. You're right. I was just waiting to see what would come after that."

"Nothing. Nothing comes after that." Because he'd learned... a lot. If he told her marriage to him wouldn't be a trap, she wouldn't believe him. And he'd be breaking his promise not to discuss the subject. "If we move fast, we'll get the horses turned out and the stalls cleaned before she gets here. But we can't—"

"I know." She squeezed his hand.

"Listen, I've been thinking. Why break up the minute my mother leaves? What difference would an extra few weeks make?"

"You want to negotiate a different cut-off date?"

"Yes, so we can make love in that stall. Several times, in fact, if it stays warm enough. I just don't see why we have to—"

"Because there will never be a right time to call it quits. If we keep seeing each other after she leaves, how do we decide something like that? Roll some dice? Throw darts at a wall calendar?"

"We can figure it out. Let me think about it." He released her hand as they stepped through the double barn door. "I'll take Silver and Toffee if you'll get Sir Eatsalot and Nugget."

"Got it." She hurried down the aisle and plucked Nugget's lead rope off a hook next to his stall.

When she'd helped him with turnout in June, her movements had been tentative. Not anymore. "You've turned into a good hand, Jenson."

"Thanks, Sullivan. How do you like it when I use both hands?"

"You know how much I like it, sassy lady."
He clipped a lead rope on Toffee and waited until
the aisle was clear. "I think Ed was hinting she'd
like you to come out and go riding with her."

"I think so, too. I'll drive over here when I
can spare the time, whether it's to ride or just to
spend time with Ed."

Couldn't get more pointed than that, could
she? "And me? After all, you said it wouldn't be like
last time. We'd be friendly."

"I'm sure we will be. See you out at the
pasture." She picked up the pace as she took Nugget
and Sir Eatsalot through the door.

He fetched Silver and led both horses out
of the barn. She was already halfway to the gate.
She had long legs, but his were longer. Catching up
was no problem.

He held his tongue until they'd turned the
horses loose and started back to the barn. "I'm not
ready to drop the subject of extending our time
together. It makes sense to me."

"Because you're thinking with the wrong
part of your anatomy."

"No, I'm not." He was listening to his heart,
but he couldn't say that.

"The longer we keep having sex, the more
involved we'll become. That'll make the shift to a
simple friendship tougher on us."

"I say it's the exact opposite. Ending it
when we're hot for each other will leave us
frustrated as hell. We need to get past the intense
phase. Then we can taper off."

"You think that will happen?"

He didn't look at her because he was about to lie through his teeth. "Sure."

She laughed. "No, you don't."

"It's possible."

"Oh, anything's possible. But you're grasping at straws because—"

"Straw. I'm grasping at straw."

"Very funny. I get it, Teague. You don't want this thrill ride to end on Sunday night."

"Do you?"

"No! But it's the right—" She squealed when he grabbed her and pulled her into his arms.

"It's not the right thing to do. But this is." Dropping the lead ropes to the ground, he kissed her, knocking off his hat and hers.

She melted against him, winding her arms around his neck and letting the lead ropes slide from her fingers. He pulled her in tight and she slackened her jaw to give him full access to her delicious mouth.

Her total surrender set off fireworks in his brain and hot lava through his body. Talking was so overrated. They communicated best when they were tangled up in each other, stoking the flames and relishing the heat.

His heartbeat pounded in his ears as he delved deep with his tongue. She moaned. Music was playing... music? *Ed's ring.*

He drew back, tried to catch his breath as he reached for the phone in his pocket. It went silent.

"Teague." Val spoke his name as if issuing a warning.

"What?"

She tilted her head.

He glanced in that direction. His mother stood about five yards away, her sunglasses perched on her head. She'd been to the salon recently. Red highlights gave a sassy look to her short brown hair.

Everything else was the same, the cherished image he carried in his head labeled *my mom.* He'd always liked that she was tall. He hadn't outgrown her until he'd turned fifteen. She preferred jeans to skirts, casual tops to silk blouses.

She was smiling, and her smile widened as she walked toward them. "You knew I was there, you rascal."

"No, ma'am, I did not." He kept his arm around Val as he turned to face the woman who'd given him life.

"You did so. I can tell by your expression. Ed sent you a text that I was on my way and you staged that kiss for my benefit."

"Didn't hear it chime." Yikes. Did she suspect the truth?

Her eyebrows rose like they did when she didn't believe him.

"Honestly, Mom, I didn't hear the chime. I did hear when Ed called, which is why I stopped kissing Val. I mean Valerie. Mom, this is Valerie Rose Jenson, my fiancée. Val, that's my mother, Madeline."

"I kinda put that together." She slipped out of his grasp and held out her hand. "It's great to meet you at last, Madeline."

His mom clasped it in both of hers. "It's a pleasure to meet you, too, Val. Can I call you that?"

"Please do. Everyone does."

His mom continued to hold Val's hand, her gaze steady. "Do you love him?"

"Yes, I do."

He almost fell over. Ah, but she had to say that. *Get a grip, dude. She's playing the part.*

He gathered up their hats and waited until his mom released Val's hand. Then he gave Val her hat, opened his arms and wrapped his mom in a tight hug. "Thanks for coming."

"Had to." She squeezed him in a mama bear hug. Then she stepped back. "That was a hot kiss."

"I was trying to make a point."

She glanced at Val. "Did he succeed?"

"Sort of. The phone interrupted his campaign."

"Reminds me of the way his father used to try and make a point with me." She turned back to him. "Now that I think about it, even though you were only three when he died, you might have memories of him trying to win an argument by kissing me."

"I wish I could say I remember, but I don't."

"Doesn't matter. Chances are your subconscious stored it away."

"Could be." And now he had questions. What had their courtship been like? How quickly had his dad proposed? Could a tendency toward love-at-first-sight be inherited?

"Oh, and Val." She switched focus. "What an awesome coincidence that we have the same middle name! When did you find out?"

"Um... I'm not sure exactly, but—"

"Never mind. Not important. Although I'm surprised Teague didn't tell me when we talked on the phone."

"I guess I don't think about middle names." He avoided looking at Val.

"Not even your own?"

"Well, of course I think about mine, since it was Dad's, but not so much with other people. You hardly ever use yours."

"That's true."

"Val doesn't, either."

"Only because Rose doesn't really fit me."

His mom nodded. "I know what you mean. I thought about keeping the initial and changing it to Reese. I like the sound of that, but I never followed through. How about you?"

Val laughed. "That's funny. I thought about Reese, too. I've always liked Reese Witherspoon."

"Same here! Hey, since we'll now be part of the same family tree, we should make a pact. If one changes to Reese, we both change. Deal?"

Val hesitated.

"Or not." His mom gave a little shrug. "I didn't mean to—"

"Deal. I'm in." Val flashed her a smile. "Pinkie swear?"

His mother returned the smile. "You know it, girlfriend." She linked little fingers with Val. "Hip bump."

As a grinning Val nudged his mom's hip, Teague let out a breath. She'd come through again. Maybe his mom suspected something. Or maybe she was simply testing her future daughter-in-law to see what she was made of.

Either way, his mother was on a fact-finding mission. He might have underestimated the difficulty of the situation.

_16_

Val had recognized a fellow teacher the minute Madeline had opened her mouth. After dealing with the pranks of her students for years, she was nobody's fool.

Did she guess this engagement wasn't real? No telling. Would she find out the truth before she left? Maybe. If she did, Val would ask forgiveness because she liked Teague's mom and wouldn't mind keeping the friendship.

"Alrighty, then." Madeline gestured toward the abandoned lead ropes lying on the ground. "What can I do to help with your barn chores. Is anybody left in there?"

"Just Herb," Val said, "but Teague and I can—"

"Of course you can, but I'm a good hand and it'll go faster if I help you muck out stalls."

"But you look so clean."

She gestured toward her clothes. "All this washes and I'm not afraid of a little dirt and sweat. My sister Julie and her husband Steve breed horses."

"Teague mentioned that." Thank God for Ed. "He said the two of you spent a lot of time out there."

"We sure did and I adored all of it. If I didn't love teaching so much I would have asked them to hire me. They did hire Teague when he was old enough, but I'm sure you know that."

"Makes sense that they would."

"They still miss you, son." Madeline glanced over at him. "They keep asking when you're moving back. I told them the other day they'll have to give up on it, now." She turned to Val. "I assume you're planning on staying here. If I thought I could pry you both away from Apple Grove, I'd—"

"Sorry, I'm not going anywhere. I'm crazy about this little town and my principal is the best."

"The *best*, huh? I can't wait to meet him. I've known some good ones over the years. Which reminds me, did Teague mention that I'd love to help you set up your room?"

"I'd be happy to have you." Thank goodness she didn't have to lie about that. Nell would enjoy Teague's mom and she'd be a hit with the girls.

"He didn't ask, did he?"

"No, but—"

"Because he's been worried about this visit from the get-go. I think he's worried that we won't get along. How ridiculous is that?"

"I wasn't worried," Teague said. "I just—"

"No, seriously, he was, Val. He tried to talk me out of coming by saying you'd be too busy getting ready for the start of school."

"Oh." He'd tried to avoid staging this deception? That was news.

He spread his arms. "What do I know? We weren't dating last August. It could have been true."

"Come on, son. You've been watching me prepare every year since you were a toddler. Just admit you were nervous about the first meeting of the two most important women in your life."

He sighed. "All right, all right. I was a little anxious. A lot was on the line."

No kidding.

"But as you can clearly see, you had nothing to worry about."

"Thank the Lord."

"Come on, then." She walked over and scooped up the lead ropes. "Let's get Herb turned out and muck us some stalls."

* * *

"Do you think she's onto us?" Val stepped out of the shower and grabbed a towel. Teague stood at the sink, bare-chested, a razor in his hand and shaving cream making him look like a very sexy Santa.

He turned. "I don't know. Sometimes I think she is and then she says something that tells me she's convinced."

"Same here." She began drying off. "I can't decide."

"I do know one thing." His gaze raked her damp body. "I'd rather stay in this house than go to the Moose tonight."

"So would I, but we're going and they'll pick us up in twenty minutes."

"Twenty minutes?" His eyes darkened. Setting the razor on the counter, he pulled a hand towel from the rack and wiped his face as he came toward her. "That's plenty of time for— dammit, there's my phone." He spun around, threw the towel on the counter and headed for the bedroom.

She continued drying off as she walked to the bathroom doorway to listen.

"Hey, Jake. How's it going, buddy?"

Jake? Wrapping herself in the towel, she padded into the bedroom to get her underwear and eavesdrop some more.

"I think she believes us." He turned, the phone to his ear and his attention on her. "Val and I were just talking about it. It's hard to tell for sure."

Draping the towel over the top of the dresser, she turned away from him and opened the top drawer.

"I don't know if that's a good idea or not, Jake."

She took out what she needed and started to close the drawer. The whisper of his bare feet alerted her so she didn't jump when he circled her ribcage, his arm tucked under the swell of her breasts.

"Well, I guess if it's just you and Millie, that wouldn't look suspicious." He drew her close and cupped her breast, squeezing gently.

She should wiggle out of his grasp. Neither of them had time for fondling. But... mm, he was an expert fondler. Warm skin, firm muscles and the rapid thud of his heart coaxed her to rest her hands on the lip of the drawer and lean into him.

"I guess Matt and Lucy would be okay, too." He nudged her backside. The worn denim of his jeans was soft, but not what lay behind it. "Yeah, she loves Lucy's artwork. But that's enough folks. We don't want to lay it on too thick."

Speaking of thick.... A sweet ache settled in her core.

"Okay, Jake. See you there. 'Bye." He laid the phone on the dresser and cradled her other breast as he nuzzled the curve of her neck. "Let's call Ed and tell her we want to drive ourselves there."

"Bad idea."

"Great idea. Then we can—"

"Look like hormonal teenagers?"

"Funny you should mention that. Perfect description of what you do to me."

She tossed her underwear on top of the dresser and covered his hands with hers. "I'm in the same boat, buster. But we're not going in separate vehicles so you and I can have a quickie." She pried his hands loose. "Go finish your shave."

Heaving a sigh, he stepped back. "I'll finish it in the shower. A very *cold* shower."

"That's the spirit." She turned and watched him walk away. Poetry in motion.

"You're ogling my ass, aren't you?"

"Don't flatter yourself."

"You are. Your breathing just changed."

"You're imagining things."

"Want to reconsider that two-vehicle plan? I can be flexible." He grasped the doorframe and looked at her over one muscled shoulder and wiggled his eyebrows. "Very flexible."

"You're incorrigible."

He laughed and ducked into the bathroom. "And you want me bad!"

Picking up her underwear, she paused to take a deep, cleansing breath. He wasn't wrong.

<u>17</u>

The venue had taken on an end-of-the-summer, anything-goes vibe. Merlin, the plush moose head mounted over the bar, sported an oversized pair of shades and a pink bubblegum cigar. His Glacier National Park souvenir cap was on backwards, rally-style.

Teague got a kick out of his mom's delighted reaction to Merlin's getup. She asked if they could eat at the bar so she could get a better view of that silly moose.

"Sounds like fun," Val said. "I've never sat at the bar."

"Then it's time you did." Ed gave her an approving nod. "And we'll be closer to our champagne source."

"Then let's do it." Teague moved to the stool closest to the entrance and propped his hip on the leather seat, staking his claim to the spot while he waited for the women to settle.

Ed made her choice, leaving two stools between her and Teague.

Val motioned to the spot next to Teague. "You should sit next to your son, Madeline."

"No, you take it. You're his fiancée."

"I'm with him all the time, so you—"

"But you're—"

"Oh, for pity's sake." Ed rolled her eyes. "Teague, will you please sit between these two women? I know you stationed yourself down there because of some gentleman's code of conduct, but you're causing a ruckus."

Val laughed. "She's right. Let me take the end spot. I promise to protect us from any threat that comes through the front door."

"Because historically there are so many." Ed made a face.

"I was just doing what comes naturally." And he could keep track of incoming members of the Brotherhood. "But I'll move." He got up and gestured to his stool. "Warmed it up for you, sweetheart." He gave her a wink for emphasis. Maybe the leftover heat would remind her of how much she liked his ass.

While the bartender laid out placemats, napkins and silverware, Ed requested a bottle of champagne and some appetizers.

Val leaned toward Teague. "When the champagne arrives, you could open it and show off your skills." She adjusted her skirt to show off her knee and a bit of thigh.

"I'd rather not." The silver buttons running down the front of her skirt were for show. Velcro held it together. Easy-off.

She ran her tongue over lips. "But you're so good at opening champagne bottles."

He shifted on his stool. If this was payback for his wink, she'd achieved her goal. "It's harder when I'm sitting down." *Oh, boy. Shouldn't have phrased it that way.*

She picked up her cue. "Is it really?" she murmured, glancing at his fly. "Must be painful."

He nudged her knee and lowered his voice. "Behave yourself."

"You started it." She mimicked his tone. "*Warmed it up for you, sweetheart.*"

He grinned. "Just stating a fact. I can't help it if—"

"Teague Wesley Sullivan, you wouldn't be harassing your lovely fiancée, would you?"

"Yes, ma'am." He smiled at Val. "But the harassing is mutual. She gives as good as she gets."

"I'm happy to hear it." She glanced at Val. "He's a really good guy, but he has a devilish streak. He can be a bit of a tease. Personally, I think that makes him more interesting."

"I'm right here, Mom."

"I know. I say those words in your presence because I love you. You need a woman who can handle that special part of you. It appears that Val's up to it."

His attempt to choke back a laugh ended in a coughing fit. Val whacked him several times on the back. Hard. He glanced sideways and managed a wheezed version of *enough.*

"Don't want you to choke to death."

He cleared his throat. "Thanks."

"I think they might have interpreted that remark differently than you meant it, Madeline." Ed's deadpan delivery sent Teague into another round of coughing.

"Oh, my God." His mom threw up her hands. "I wasn't referring to sex. I was only trying to clarify that a little gentle friction can be a good... I mean, a healthy back-and-forth between two... oh, never mind!"

Ed lost it, leaning on the bar as she laughed until she was gasping for breath.

A soft hiss from behind the bar was followed by the bartender raising a bottle with vapor drifting from the open neck. He quickly filled four glasses and tucked the bottle into an ice bucket sitting next to Ed's place at the bar.

"I desperately need some of that." His mom grabbed one of the flutes and took a gulp.

Ed straightened and wiped the tears from her eyes. "Me, too. I can't remember the last time I've laughed that hard." She picked up a glass, took a sip and grinned at his mom. "You need to visit more often."

"That sounds lovely. But I wasn't trying to be funny. I wanted to make a point. I can't imagine where those phrases came from."

Teague swallowed a fizzy mouthful of champagne. "How about that *Fun in the Sack* party you went to Sunday night?"

"You could be right. The jokes were flying at that party, which was exactly what you thought it was, by the way. I was going to bring some of the items with me on this trip, but I changed my mind."

"That's too bad." Ed made a sad face. "I would have liked to see what's current."

"Next time, then. I was thinking they'd be fun prizes for the bridal shower." She turned to Val.

"But I'm not pushing for a date, I promise. Just when you're ready."

"Thanks, but it's a great idea for a shower prize." She sent him a sly glance. "I haven't been to one of those parties in a while. Might be some new stuff out."

Was she implying she had a stash of toys? One more subject to discuss when they were alone. *Alone.* The prospect beckoned to him, a mirage in the desert.

"I think she should bring them next time she visits, whether a shower's scheduled or not." Ed pulled the bottle out of the ice bucket and topped off her glass. "I'm passing this down the line. We need to kill this bottle so we can order another."

"Good plan." His mom took some and handed the bottle to Teague, who filled Val's glass and then his own.

His mom held up her flute. "Here's to creating joyful friction."

"Mom!"

She laughed. "I got myself into it and I'll get myself out. Where do you suppose you learned how to tease?"

Val gave her a thumbs-up. "Nice job, Madeline." She touched her glass to his mother's, Ed's, and finally his. She took a sip and set down her flute.

"We should probably order." Ed picked up a menu. "I don't know why I even look at this. I know what I want. The Moose is the only time I indulge myself in a good old-fashioned burger with all the trimmings."

"I could go for that," his mom said.

Val nodded. "Suits me."

"Me, too." Teague gave their order to the bartender and turned to her. "The band's tuning up. Care to dance?"

"You read my mind."

He stood, but as he held out his hand to help her down, Jake and Millie came in and headed straight for the bar.

Jake took the conversational lead. "We just wanted to say hello to your mom, Teague, old buddy. Hey, Mrs. Sullivan. How're you doing?"

"Great! Good to see you, Jake. And it's Madeline, remember?"

"Yes, ma'am, I do recollect that now. You met my wife Millie last time, didn't you?"

"I sure did. You guys weren't married, then. Teague told me you did the deed on New Year's Eve."

"We did," Millie said. "God help us."

"Bold choice, and smart, too. Now you'll have no excuse for forgetting your anniversary."

"Indeed." Jake smiled. "Go big or go home. Which brings us to the next topic." He laid one hand on Val's shoulder and the other on Teague's. "Congrats, you two. Happy news."

"Thanks, Jake. I'm a lucky guy."

"You are, indeed. Val, if you need any help keeping this cowboy in line, let me know."

"You'll be the first, Jake."

"Jake can be the second," his mom said. "I should be the first. If you have complaints, Val, come straight to the manufacturer."

Jake chuckled. "Good one. I'm stealing it for future use."

Teague stared at him. "Is that your way of saying—"

"Oh, no, no!" He waved both hands in the air. "Trust me, when Millie and I make that announcement, we'll put it up in flashing neon."

"And if you don't, Henri will. But dude, you won't have a chance to use my mom's zinger for another twenty-five or thirty years."

"I know. It'll still be good. Except come to think of it, there won't be any complaints." He grinned. "My kids will be perfect."

Millie started laughing. "Oh, yeah. Of course they will."

"Wait and see. I'll transfer all my hard-won knowledge for creating a blissful marriage. Their spouses will reap the benefits. No complaints."

"Val's not going to have complaints, either." Teague looped an arm around her waist. "I'll make sure of that."

"Whoa, buddy." Jake nudged back his hat. "I was mostly kidding."

"I'm not."

"I advise against going for zero complaints. You'll crash and burn for sure. I'd shoot for an average per month, maybe something in the teens."

Millie flashed a smile at her husband. "Goose it up a notch or two, honey bunch, and you've got it about right."

"In the twenties, then. If you get into the thirties, you're heading for trouble, but keep it below that and you'll be okay."

"If you say so." Teague wasn't going to argue with Jake and Millie, because in their case, those stats might be true. But if by some miracle he ended up married to Val, she would have zero complaints. He'd see to it.

_18_

After Jake and Millie left, Madeline glanced at Teague. "Jake's a hoot."

"Yes, he is."

"That was very nice of him and Millie, coming over to congratulate you."

Val went on alert. They'd said they just wanted a chance to say hello to her. The congratulations had been almost an afterthought. Had Madeline figured out the meet-and-greet was staged?

Maybe not. Don't get paranoid, girl.

Teague picked up his champagne. "I'm not surprised they showed up."

Oh, Teague. Val swallowed a laugh.

He calmly sipped his bubbly. "The Buckskin gang's very happy about this."

"Not as happy as I am. I was beginning to wonder if you'd find what you were looking for." Her gaze moved past him. "Clearly he did. I'm hoping you did, too, Val."

"Absolutely."

"I realize your engagement is only days old, but have you talked at all about a wedding date?"

Just her luck that Madeline directed that question to her instead of Teague. "We haven't talked about it much. I'm a little wedding-phobic."

"And I'm happy to wait." Teague reached over and squeezed her hand.

Ed leaned around Madeline and made eye contact. "Take my advice and enjoy a nice long engagement, Val. Don't push it. You'll know when the time is right."

"Thanks, Ed." She could kiss that woman. And Teague, too. Well, she'd like to do more than kiss him, but—

"Will you ladies excuse us, please?" He stood and offered his hand. "I'd like to claim that dance with my fiancée."

"By all means." His mother beamed at them. "Wonderful idea."

Once they were on the dance floor, Val settled into his arms with a sigh of relief. "Nice."

"Yes, ma'am." He tucked her in for a slow song.

She nestled closer and laid her cheek against the soft cotton of his Western shirt. "Did you hear Millie call Jake *honey bunch*?"

"I did."

"I need to call you Teague-a-rooney. To strengthen our case."

"No, you don't. We're doing okay so far."

"I wish I could tell what your mom's thinking."

"I have a pretty good idea." He massaged the small of her back. "She knows something isn't adding up, but she can't deny our strong connection."

"I can't, either."

"Tell me about it. I can't forget how good you felt while I was talking to Jake on the phone. I don't know how I managed to carry on a conversation."

"Because you're a cool customer. I about died when you said *I'm not surprised they showed up.*" She lifted her head to look up at him. "How did you say that with a straight face?"

"Wasn't easy, but that meeting was too on the nose. I was afraid it would be when Jake outlined his plan. She wasn't totally buying it. I figured if I hit it head-on by saying something like that, she might decide she was imagining things."

"She's very smart."

"Yes, she is."

"What made you think you could outwit her?"

He smiled. "I'm smart, too. And my fiancée is even smarter."

"Thank you for that, but I've never done anything like this before. I'm afraid if she gets me cornered, I'll sing like a bird."

His gaze softened. "Don't be afraid. You always have the option of telling her. If a time comes when you feel you need to, then do it."

"But I'll get you in big trouble."

"My own doing. Not your problem."

She locked her hands behind his neck and swayed to the music. "I want to kiss you right now."

"I want to kiss you, too. But that will lead to things that aren't appropriate on a dance floor."

"You don't think we could have a nice easy kiss and keep it at that?"

His sexy grin gave her the answer.

"You know what? We need to be able to kiss like that. Nell and Zeke do. It's romantic and it will help convince your mother."

"Good point, but I'm not sure I can—"

"Sure you can. Lean down here and give me a gentle kiss. Expand your repertoire."

"A gentle kiss is already in my repertoire, thank you very much."

"Then how come you've never given me one?"

"I have. I guess you missed it."

"When?"

He lowered his voice. "After we've had sweaty sex, not before. We're in the before-times, when my thoughts are on ripping off that skirt and tossing you down on my bed."

Her skin flushed. "You're not helping. Is your mother watching us?"

"Don't know. I'll check." He turned her in a lazy circle. "Yep, she is."

"I'm telling you, it's a good idea."

"All right, let's try it. Shut your eyes and lift your chin."

Eyes closed and face turned upward, she ran her tongue over her lips and waited. For some stupid reason her heart was pounding. Ridiculous. It was just a kiss to make the engagement look real.

Okay, not only that. She craved the sensation of his lips on hers. A mild kiss was better than nothing, right?

His warm breath caressed her mouth a second before his lips, soft as velvet, brushed hers.

Slowly he applied subtle pressure, not too much, just enough to make the intimate connection.

He tightened his arms, bringing her closer, but his kiss remained easy, undemanding, as if he cherished this moment, cherished her. The music and the chatter from the crowd faded.

A lightness filled her, as if she could float, as if she and Teague were adrift on a cloud, alone in a world of gauzy light and swirling pastels. Delicious. A subtle hum of desire undulated under the surface, a ripple of awareness. Just enough.

Gradually he lifted his lips.

No. Don't stop. This is amazing.

"All done." His voice sounded normal.

The music and the noise of the dinner crowd returned, dissolving her hazy watercolor world. Gone. Damn it. She opened her eyes.

His expression was impossible to read. Had he experienced that floaty, drifting-on-a cloud stuff? Maybe not. Better not mention it.

She cleared her throat and got her bearings. "See? We kissed and didn't end up rolling around on the floor tearing each other's clothes off."

"Imagine that."

"The music's stopped."

"Yes, ma'am." He glanced toward the bar. "And our food just arrived. Ready to go eat?"

"Sounds like a plan."

He took her hand and threaded his fingers through hers as they walked back to the bar.

And there it was again, not as strong but still messing with her, that darned floaty thing.

<u>19</u>

During the meal, Val spilled catsup on her shirt and excused herself to go clean it off in the restroom. Ed, a whiz at stain removal, went with her.

The minute they left, Teague's mom put down her hamburger and faced him. "I'm relieved to find out your relationship is based on more than sex."

"What brought that on?"

"Your kiss on the dance floor."

Val had been right. And she'd put him through hell. He'd nearly mastered the role of a carefree lover only interested in a good time. Then she'd asked him to switch gears and give her the kiss of a man deeply in love.

Oh, he could do it. Had ached to do it for months. Those few moments had been heaven.

Re-entry had been rough. He'd been a split-second away from saying *I love you*. Locking that down, especially when she gave him a dreamy-eyed look, had twisted his insides into a knot that was just now loosening.

"Nothing wrong with having a healthy sex life." His mom's gaze twinkled. "I'm just glad that's not all you have going for you."

"It's not." But it was the primary thing he had going for him the next four nights.

"Considering how you feel about each other, I can't figure out why you tried to keep me from coming here."

Oh, boy. How to field that comment?

"Blame it on me." Val arrived in the nick of time and slipped onto the stool to his right. "He knew I was a little freaked about being engaged, and he was worried that having you come so soon would stress me out."

"Oh. I guess that makes sense." She glanced at him. "You could have told me that instead of making up an excuse about school."

"I can see why he didn't." Ed poked her way into the conversation. "He was being protective of Val. He didn't want to make her out to be a head case."

"Okay." His mom nodded. "Good point." She looked over at Val. "Did I stress you out, honey? Because if I did—"

"I was a little agitated at first, but scooping poop together took care of that."

His mom grinned. "It's the great leveler, isn't it?"

"That's what I've always maintained." Ed polished off her champagne. "Nothing better than— oh, listen to that. *Boot Scootin' Boogie.* Let's get out there, Madeline." She turned to Teague and Val. "You guys coming?"

"Not me," Val said. "I'd rather sit and watch you two." She turned her stool to face the dance floor.

"Great idea." Teague spun his around, too, as his mom and Ed headed off to join the other dancers. "Did I tell you my mom's a tap dancer?"

"You did not."

"Has been since she was a kid. She's the driving force behind the Tottering Tappers, a bunch of retired teachers."

"That explains why she's killing that line dance."

"Yeah." He laughed as she added a shimmy to the action. "I've always loved watching her dance. She looks so happy."

"She does. Will she forgive us when she finds out the truth?"

"I've been thinking about that. If we get through this episode, I'll fly up to Eugene in a month or so and tell her in person."

"Good idea. Put in a good word for me, will you?"

"Absolutely. And thanks for coming to my rescue just now. I was floundering. Between you and Ed, you smoothed things out."

"I'm glad the timing was good."

"And you were right about the kiss." Amazing that he could talk about it so calmly. Maybe because he was concentrating on the dancing and not looking at her.

"Oh? She mentioned it?"

"First thing she said after you and Ed went to work on the ketchup stain. She's relieved that our relationship is based on more than sex."

"Do you think we've passed the danger point and she's bought into it?"

"Maybe. In case I haven't said it enough, I'm grateful that you agreed to this plan." He nudged back his hat. "When I first asked, I figured my chances of convincing you were zero to none."

"The truth is, if you'd made a move when you were at my house, I would've caved immediately."

His pulse rate picked up. "I had a hunch that was the case."

"Why didn't you?"

"Wouldn't have been fair to press my advantage. You had to make the first move, not me."

She smiled. "Noble of you. Did you expect me to show up at your house?"

"Nope. That was a surprise. A good one."

"I've never done anything like that before."

"I'm honored to be the first." And he desperately wanted to be the last. The thought of her with another man gnawed at his vitals. Could be he'd have to get used to it. "That dance was the sexiest—" He paused, his focus shifting to the front door. "Matt and Lucy just came in."

"I'm glad your mom isn't here. We need to stop them from doing the congratulations bit."

"Right." He stood. "Hey, you two. Thanks for showing up, but—"

"Your mom's not here," Lucy said with a laugh. "Hi, Val. Bad timing, huh?"

"Great timing." She gestured toward the dance floor. "She's out there with Ed, which gives us a chance to tell you not to bother with the congratulations thing."

Lucy's eyes widened. "She's onto you?"

"Not yet, but she's still looking for holes in the story. Jake and Millie stopping by made her more suspicious, not less."

"See?" Lucy turned toward her husband. "That's what I said. I've gotten to know her better since she started collecting my art. She's sharp. She'd recognize a setup." She glanced at Teague. "Where do things stand, now?"

"Not too bad. But Val's right. Another couple showing up to offer congrats could set us back."

"I'd still like to say hello." Lucy checked out the dancers. "We can stay here until they get back. Then I'll make it all about me wanting to connect with Madeline about a sketch she wants. She's commissioned one of Sir Eatsalot. She thinks he's adorable."

"Which he is," Val said. "Ask her if you can make a print of the original, because I'd love to buy one."

"I'm sure she'd say yes." When the music stopped, Lucy surveyed the dance floor. "Here comes Ed, but Madeline stayed to talk to some guy."

"She did?" Teague swung around and zeroed in on his mother. She was having a cozy chat with a gray-haired dude. "Who's that?"

Lucy shook her head. "Haven't a clue. Matt?"

"Might be the banker who gave me the loan to buy Thunder."

"He's vice-president of the bank." Ed arrived, a big smile on her face. "I introduced them after the line dance."

Teague blinked. "Why would you do that?"

"All part of my grand plan." The music started up again. "Are they dancing? I don't want her to catch me looking."

"They're dancing." Teague was riveted. "And she's laughing."

"He has a good sense of humor."

"How'd you work this? She never wanted to before. She'd dance with me, but that was it."

"He's a plant. I told him I'd get her out on the floor for a line dance and he had to grab his opportunity right after it ended."

"When was this?" He flicked a glance at Ed before returning his attention to his mom and the banker guy. Uneasiness gripped him.

"Day before yesterday. He's not the only one."

"*What*?" He turned to stare at her.

"I lined up three very nice men and asked them to rotate and make sure she got plenty of time on the floor. I sent them her picture and told them a little something about her. It was easy. She's a beautiful, intelligent woman with a lot to offer. And she can dance like nobody's business."

"You're *matchmaking*?" His gut clenched.

"Not at all. These are local guys. She's not moving, at least we all hope not."

"Then what the h—"

"I just want her to remember what it's like to flirt and have fun with the opposite sex."

"Why?"

"In case I'm right that she just needs a little nudge to reconsider the idea of dating." Ed's gaze was as calm as a cloudless summer sky.

"Exactly when were you going to tell me this?"

"I just did." She looked over at Matt and Lucy. "You're skipping the congratulations speech, right?"

"Yes, ma'am." Matt sounded like he was about to bust out laughing. "And your strategy is brilliant, by the way."

"I wouldn't call it *brilliant.*" Outrageous was more like it. He got a kick out of Ed's talent for outrageous behavior. Except when it involved his mom. He kept sneaking peeks at the dance floor. "I wish you'd run it by me."

"Why? She's your mother but she's my girlfriend. Which makes me way better qualified to judge whether this is a good idea or not. Would you have thought of it?"

"No." *And hell no.*

"And even if you had thought of it, you wouldn't have the contacts to make it happen. I do."

"I just wish you'd—"

"I didn't tell you beforehand because I suspected you wouldn't be crazy about the idea."

"I'm not."

"Don't you want her to stop focusing on your love life?"

"Yes, but—"

"This is the classic answer to your problem." She swept a hand toward the dance floor. "Encourage her to focus on her own."

20

On the way home, Val held hands with a distracted Teague in the darkened back seat of Ed's fancy truck. She'd initiated the hand-holding as a gesture of support. Poor guy had been thrown for a loop by Ed's bold move and his mom's enthusiastic reaction.

For the remainder of the evening, he'd behaved like a spectator at a tennis match. His attention switched constantly between her and his mother, who was mostly on the dance floor.

Talking to him at the bar had become complicated. Several times she'd had to repeat something because he'd been totally focused on the dancers. Out on the floor, he'd bungled his usually smooth moves and twice he'd stepped on her toes.

Yes, it was funny, but touching, too. Clearly he didn't know what to make of a situation he'd never encountered and hadn't a clue how to handle.

Ed had continued to reassure him that everything was fine, that none of these guys would act inappropriately. The few times his energized mother had returned to her seat at the bar, she'd laughingly told him to relax. She might as well have asked him to transform into a different person, one who didn't have a protective streak a mile wide.

Now that they were headed back, his attention was no longer divided. She might have his hand, but the rest of him was fully occupied with the conversation in the front seat.

Madeline's excitement bubbled over like a shaken bottle of champagne. "That was the most fun I've had in years. It's obvious you recruited those guys to dance with me, but I don't care, because they genuinely had a good time and so did I."

"I didn't have to work very hard, toots. You're an easy sell."

"Hey," Teague said. "That's my mother you're talking about."

She turned around and flapped a hand at him. "Take it easy, son. I'm flattered that Ed could find three good-looking, intelligent men who wanted to dance with me."

"You danced with more than three guys."

"Yes, she did!" Ed chortled with glee. "They came out of the woodwork. I loved seeing them jockeying for position. You looked good out there, Madeline. Didn't she, Val?"

"Sure did. You're a wonderful dancer. I wish you were staying longer so you could teach me some steps." Had she really said that?

"Thank you." Madeline gave her a smile. "It was quite the ego boost. The ones Ed picked are excellent dancers, so that helped. Most of the others weren't. But they were sweet and I couldn't bear to turn them down."

"The one with the red shirt didn't look much older than me." Disapproval gave an edge to his voice.

"Up close he doesn't," Madeline said. "He keeps in shape, so he looks younger from a distance. I'd say he's in his mid-forties."

"That's not a bad age gap." Ed flashed her a grin. "You could pass for early fifties."

Teague's fingers tightened. "I thought this wasn't about matchmaking?"

His mom scooted around so she could look at him. "It's not, son. I doubt I'll ever see that man again. Or any of them. Well, except Cliff, the banker. We have a lunch date for Saturday."

Ed slapped the steering wheel. "Booya!"

"I hope you don't mind, Teague. I'm here to see you, of course, but—"

"He has his work to do, don't you, Teague?"

"Yes, ma'am. And I don't mind, but I don't see the point."

"He sponsors a clothing drive every year and he wants to ask me about the one I run in Eugene. It's not so much a date as a chance to share information."

Ed glanced at her. "And you also get to have a nice lunch with an attractive man."

"I suppose, but that's not my motivation."

Teague's grip relaxed.

"But if the lunch goes well..." Ed paused for emphasis. "I'm thinking you could find similar attractive men in Eugene who'd like to have lunch."

His fingers tensed.

"Oh, for heaven's sake, Ed. Is that where you're going with this?"

Val had a perfect view of Ed's jawline illuminated in the lights from the dash. Judging from the muscle twitching there, Ed wasn't happy with Madeline's question.

"Why not?" Her tone revealed her frustration. "You'd have no trouble finding them in a bigger town like Eugene. I'll bet that place is crawling with great guys your age who would love—"

"But I don't want a great guy. I had one, and nobody will ever measure up to Wes. I can't imagine sharing a house and my life with anyone else."

Ed's beleaguered sigh said it all. If she hadn't been driving, she likely would have banged her head against the steering wheel.

"I look forward to having lunch with Cliff, but I look forward to having lunch with the Tottering Tappers, too. I have a social life. I don't need to have lunch with some guy just to spice things up."

"A conversation with a single man who's interested in you is totally different from one with girlfriends."

Teague leaned forward. "Mom, I think you should do what feels right. If dating sounds like fun, then do it. But if you're happy with things as they are—"

"I'm not implying that she's unhappy." Ed put on her turn signal and turned onto the ranch road. "But it's possible she could be happier if she branched out a little."

"Or I could buy myself a whole lot of trouble."

"Not necessarily. Look at Henri and Ben. Weren't they amazing tonight?"

"Incredible." Val was happy to dive into the conversation on that topic. She wouldn't have touched the other one with a ten-foot pole. "I loved how they cleared the floor." Same age as her parents. Totally different behavior. "Aren't they newlyweds?"

Ed nodded. "Got hitched last month. We all expected them to throw a big bash, but they went the other way, small and sweet."

"It was the right call," Teague said. "A simple wedding suited them."

Of course he'd been invited. If she hadn't broken up with him, she would have been invited, too. Nell, the soul of tact, hadn't mentioned the ceremony, but Val had heard someone talking about it in the hair salon.

"It definitely was the right call." Ed slowed as a family of raccoons crossed the road. "I'm not ashamed to say I cried all through the ceremony. Anyway, Madeline, my point is that like you, she thought nobody could measure up to Charley, but she finally gave Ben a chance. You see the results."

"She was lucky. Ben seems like a terrific guy."

"For all you know, there's a Ben Malone living in Eugene."

"Needle, meet haystack."

Teague chuckled.

"You are one stubborn lady." Ed shook her head.

"Hey, if you're so big on this idea, what about you?" Madeline glanced over at Ed. "Why aren't you having lunch and playing footsie with a dashing octogenarian?"

She laughed. "They're out there, but they're not thick on the ground, especially in a small town. I may have to go younger to find someone my speed."

"Then take one of these guys after I'm gone."

"I just might." She drove past the main house and pulled up in front of Teague's place. "I'll be serving breakfast at the same time as I did today, if you want to come up after you feed."

"Thanks, Ed." Teague took off his seat belt and opened the door. "That sounds great."

Madeline turned toward the back seat. "I had plans to help you guys feed, but I drank a little too much champagne tonight. I'll do it day after tomorrow, for sure."

"No worries." Val squeezed Madeline's shoulder before she took Teague's hand and stepped out of the car. "We've got this."

"What Val said, Mom. Thanks for driving, Ed. We'll see you both in the morning."

His mom and Ed called out their goodnights as he closed the door. Then he laced his fingers through hers and started toward the porch as Ed circled around and drove away.

She lobbed an innocuous comment into the silence. "Quite a night."

He drew in a breath. "Yes, ma'am, you could say that."

"I gather you're not pleased with Ed's campaign."

"I'm sure she means well, but if Mom says she's happy with her life, why encourage her to change it?"

"I kind of go along with Ed's logic, though. Even I can tell that your mom's a very romantic person."

"Well, sure, but—"

"I think Ed might have figured out why your mom's so eager for you to get married. I understand the situation much better now." And him. He was as much a romantic as his mother.

"Ed thinks she's trying to live vicariously through me." He climbed the steps, holding tight to her hand.

"Yes."

"And maybe it's the safer route for her."

"Safer isn't always better. In fact, usually it's—"

"But perfect matchups don't come along every day. Like she said, *needle, meet haystack.* She's not going to settle for second-best."

She hesitated. "I'd like to ask you something. But you might not want to hear it."

"I probably know what it is."

"Maybe not."

"Oh, I think I do." He ushered her through the door into the darkened living room and closed the door. Then he paused. "I'll admit it was weird seeing her out there dancing with guys I don't know. I didn't like it."

"I could tell." She took his other hand and gazed at him. His face was mostly in shadow. "Why not?"

"I don't want her to get hurt."

"I'm sure you don't. She doesn't want you to get hurt, either."

"After tonight, I have a better idea what she goes through watching me. I wanted to have a long chat with every one of those ol' boys and let them know the consequences if they stepped out of line."

She smiled. "You showed great restraint."

"Yep."

"Any other reason you didn't like it?"

"That's pretty much it."

No, it isn't. But she wouldn't challenge him. He might not be able to admit the deeper reason.

"The only other person she's danced with besides me is my Uncle Steve at my cousin's wedding. He never has too much to drink but he was schnockered that night. My cousin married a great guy after almost running off with a loser and Uncle Steve was so happy. He danced with everybody."

"And now you want to marry a great woman so you can watch your Uncle Steve get schnockered again." A part of her wanted to see it, too.

"Yes, ma'am." He pulled her close. "That's my secret plan. It's all about my Uncle Steve."

"This is cozy, being here in the living room in the dark."

"Wanna stay here and make love on the couch?"

"Not really." Too romantic.

"You're sure? It's chilly enough to make a small fire."

"But the couch isn't in front of the fireplace anymore."

"You're right. I forgot. I could move it."

"No, don't." *You'll only have to move it back when I'm gone.*

Perversely, what she wanted was another kiss like the one he'd given her on the dance floor. It seemed like exactly the right ending for this tender moment as the quiet house wrapped around them like a hug.

"You're sure you don't want me to move the couch? It'll only take a minute."

"I'm sure." If she asked him for that kiss, they'd cross a line into territory she'd labeled off-limits. And it would be all on her.

Instead she wiggled out of his arms and backed away. The glow from the porchlight came through the front window and it sparkled on her skirt's row of silver buttons. "Your big ol' bed's way better for what I have in mind." As she ripped off her skirt, the harsh scratch of Velcro instantly changed the mood. She tossed it aside.

His breath caught. "You've been wearing a thong under there?

"Yessir."

"Good thing I didn't know."

"You do, now, cowboy." She moved backward toward the hall. "And I'm gonna let you take it off with your teeth."

21

Using his teeth to take off Val's thong led to giving her a love bite on the tender inside of her thigh, just a little one. She liked it. Wanted more.

He got into it, nipping his way over every delicious inch of her sleek body. He was ready to explode when she turned the tables on him, insisting he lie down and let her do the same.

She made a feast of him, taking great liberties with his package. Talk about erotic. He was on fire, barely had the presence of mind to fetch a condom from the bedside drawer and hand it to her.

She was panting as she rolled it on. "I hate to cover up my favorite chew toy."

"You'll be very sorry if you don't." He clenched his jaw against the orgasm pushing hard against his iron control.

Snapping the condom in place, she straddled him. "Cork about to pop?"

"Yes, ma'am." He grasped her around the waist. "I'd be obliged if you'd—"

"Turn me loose, cowboy. I know what I'm doing."

Evidently she did. In seconds she had him yelling colorful curse words as she rode them both to a shattering climax.

Gradually his world stopped spinning. He gazed up at her. Hands braced on his sweaty chest, head thrown back and breasts quivering, she fulfilled every fantasy he'd had or would have. Love swept through him, a cleansing wind that brought clarity.

He didn't have to say it. He knew it and that was enough. What he needed for this moment was a joke. And he had one.

Needle, meet haystack. He chuckled.

She tilted her head to meet his gaze. "Do I look funny?"

"You look amazing, all flushed and shiny with sweat."

Her smile exposed those pearly whites that had driven him almost to madness. "Women aren't supposed to be shiny with sweat. We gleam and glow."

"Whatever you're supposed to do, it's a great look on you. I wasn't laughing about that."

"What, then?'

"That needle and haystack thing. You could make it sexual."

"I'm sure *you* could. You have sex on the brain right now. I doubt it was meant that way in the beginning."

"I'm sure not. But if you'll be kind enough to lift your haystack, I'll tend to my needle."

She groaned. "Now I'll think of that every time I hear the phrase."

"Gonna let me up, lady of the gleam?"

"Yes." She carefully eased away from him. "But you're a naughty man, Teague Wesley Sullivan, taking a common expression and making it something else entirely."

"But you like that about me." Holding onto the condom, he swung his feet over the side and stood.

"Sad to say, I do. Now get out of here."

He escaped without giving her a gentle, loving kiss, something he'd done a couple of times the night before. He'd gotten away with it then. He couldn't take the chance now.

When he came back, she'd plumped the pillows and straightened the sheets. She lay on the far side of the bed under the covers, her head propped on her hand. She'd left plenty of room for him.

He'd walked into this room multiple times when she'd been in bed waiting for him, her gaze hot. This wasn't one of those times. "Much neater in here than when I left."

Her smile was tentative. "I hate to say it, but I'm wiped out. Tomorrow we have the riding lesson with the girls and I want to be on my game. Would you think I'm a loser if I suggested we get some sleep?"

"I'd think you're a smart lady who knows her limits." He switched off the light, pulled back the covers and climbed in, rolling to his side to face her but leaving a space. An automatic nightlight in the bathroom came on. She was shadowy at first, but as his eyes adjusted, he could see well enough to gauge her expression.

This was new and he had to learn how she preferred to go into this routine. They'd never deliberately settled down to sleep. Usually they'd dropped off in the middle of a make-out session, or he'd returned from the bathroom to find her off to dreamland.

Her gaze was adorably earnest. "It's kind of funny. I've spent time in your bed, but I haven't exactly *slept* with you, I mean, deliberately rolled over, said goodnight, and drifted off."

"I know." That behavior belonged to committed couples who slept peacefully side-by-side, confident many more nights of lovemaking were ahead of them.

"We've always been so hungry for each other that it wasn't a priority."

"True." For him, it still wasn't. The clock was ticking. But she was tired and honest enough to say so. "How do want to… set up?"

"I don't know. I've never stayed with a man long enough to figure that out. The only person I've shared a bed with is my sister."

"I think this will be different."

She grinned. "I hope so. She kicks."

"Maybe I do, too. Who knows?"

"If you do, expect an elbow in the ribs."

"My ribs can take it. Other parts, not so much."

"My parents used to roll up a blanket and put it down the middle of the bed to keep us from fighting."

"We can skip that. I'm a lover, not a fighter."

"We could just go to sleep, each on our own side."

"Is that the side you want? If it isn't, I'll switch with you."

"This is the one I took when my sister and I shared a double bed. We only did it on vacation at my grandparents' house." She made a face. "I didn't like sharing. Sometimes I'd sleep on the floor so I could have my own space."

Should he give her the bed and take the couch? Nope. Jasper the dog would do that. "I'd be happy to—"

"You're not giving me your bed. That would be wrong."

"Wasn't going to. I'm taking the bed, but I have extra blankets if you want to sleep on the floor."

Her eyes widened and then she grinned. "You really have changed."

"Thanks for noticing."

"I want to give this a shot, but I may be lousy at it."

He shrugged. "Same here. We won't know until we try." Time to cut to the chase. "I have a suggestion."

"What?"

"Spooning."

"Won't a position like that lead to... things?"

"Not if you're exhausted. I promise not to fondle." He lifted the covers. "Roll over here and turn your back to me. Let's see how it feels. If you think it's too sexy, we'll do something else."

"Okay. Here goes." She accomplished the maneuver easily, tucking into the curve of his body as if she'd been doing it all her life. "How's that?"

Perfect. Incredible. As if we were two halves of a whole. "Works for me." He slid his arm around her waist and flattened his palm against her stomach. "Mind if I do this?"

Her breath hitched. "Feels cozy."

"Mm-hm." He willed his cock to behave and his breath to stay steady.

"I can feel your heart beating. It's going kind of fast."

"It'll settle down when the novelty wears off."

She bunched the pillow under her head. "I think I like this."

"Me, too." Like it? He'd sacrifice all his worldly possessions for the privilege of holding her this way for the rest of his life.

"Good night, Teague."

"Good night, Val."

Gradually she relaxed against him. Her breathing grew shallow... and she was asleep. She must have been dead on her feet. Slight twitches and little snuffles told him she was likely dreaming.

He needed sleep, too. He'd been on the same schedule as Val. He'd be teaching that lesson tomorrow and dealing with four high-energy little girls.

But he didn't want to go under, didn't want to let go of the deep joy filling his chest as he held her. She was a wild thing, desperate to keep her freedom, terrified of being trapped in a miserable cage like her parents and her sister.

If he'd been patient enough to discover that back in June... but he barreled ahead, a bull in a china shop. Fixing what he'd broken had looked impossible a week ago. Not so impossible while she lay in his arms tonight. All he needed was time. Would she give it to him?

22

Val stepped out of the shower and plucked a towel from the rack. The aroma of coffee brewing drifted in from the kitchen, thanks to Teague. He'd slipped out of bed first, pulled on his jeans and headed for the kitchen to start it.

She'd taken her cue and jumped in the shower. This was her reward — standing on the thick bathmat drying off while enjoying the view.

Let others rave about gorgeous sunsets, majestic mountains or pristine beaches. A broad-shouldered, shirtless cowboy stroking white foam from his square jaw beat them all.

He glanced at her and smiled. "Morning, sunshine. Sleep well?"

"Like a log. You?"

"The same. I— hang on, was I too rough?" Putting down his razor, he closed the distance in two strides, a frown drawing his dark brows together. "Hold still, looks like you have a bruise."

She pressed the towel against her chest as he tilted her head to one side and swore softly. "Didn't mean to do that." He lightly touched the side of her throat. "Does that hurt?"

"No, but if you want to kiss it and make it better, go right ahead. Then we can check the rest of me in case I need that attention elsewhere."

"You have *more*?"

"That depends. If you're going to kiss it and make it better, then maybe I—"

"Let me look at you." He pulled the towel from her hands and dropped it to the floor.

"I like where this is going."

"I'm serious, damn it." He held out her arms as he began his inspection. "If I left a bunch of bruises, I'll never forgive myself."

"I doubt you'll find anything, but maybe I should check you out for damage. I was pretty aggressive with your—"

"Never mind. I'm fine." He lowered her hands. "Turn around, please."

She rotated in place.

"Aw, hell." He dropped to his knees. "You have another one right here." He lightly brushed her left cheek.

"Ask me if I care."

"*I* care."

"Like I said, if you'd like to kiss it and make it better…"

"Can't take the chance." He stood. "Evidently I go crazy when my mouth contacts your delectable backside." He turned her to face him. "I'm sorry I hurt you. I'll—"

"Teague." She grasped his arms and met his troubled gaze. "I asked you to keep it up."

"I know, but—"

"I even begged you not to stop, just like you urged me on. If I'd been in actual pain, I would have told you. I kind of like having those souvenirs. Reminds me of what a hot time we had."

The deep groove of his frown slowly relaxed. "If you say so. But next time I'll dial it back."

She ran her palm over his lightly furred chest. "Not if I can help it."

His eyes narrowed. "I see."

"I like it when you go full steam." She massaged his chest. "It's thrilling for me. If something's too much, I'll let you know. I trust you to do the same."

"Yes, ma'am." He sucked in a breath and captured her hand, ending the massage. "Are you all dried off, now?"

"Mostly. Except for this one pesky area."

He groaned. "We have to go feed."

"I know." Freeing her hand, she stepped around him and walked into the bedroom. "I'm just priming the pump for later." She opened the top dresser drawer and pulled out underwear.

"I knew that." He muttered something else, clearly talking to himself. Or his buddy below his belt.

She dressed quickly and was heading out the door to check on Florence when the shower stopped and he called to her. "Do you think fourth-grade girls know about hickeys?"

"Depends on the girl. But I'm glad you mentioned it. I'll wear a bandana around my neck today just to be safe."

"Thank you. Those girls...."

"Don't worry, Teague." She smiled. "I've got your back."

* * *

Breakfast at Ed's was blissfully free of talk about Madeline's dating prospects, and for that Val was grateful. After breakfast, Madeline helped muck out the stalls and she used it as a chance to gather background on the four girls she'd be meeting that afternoon.

Her insightful questions impressed the heck out of Val. Teague's mom clearly was in the right profession.

"They sound fabulous," she said as they finished spreading clean straw in each stall. "I've had kids like that over the years and it's always a joy. Those are the ones who come back and visit you when they're adults."

"What fun that will be! I can't wait to see how my students turn out. These four, especially. They're gonna be stars in whatever they choose."

"It's so rewarding to think you had a little part in helping them get there. I remember one kid who—" Madeline's phone chimed. "That's my alarm. I need to freshen up before Ed and I go to Henri's for lunch."

"I missed that memo." Teague leaned on his pitchfork.

"I forgot to tell you. She called right before breakfast and said she wanted to piggyback onto the riding lesson and grab us for lunch at her house."

"Nice."

"She's checking with Jake to see if he can give us a Raptors Rise tour after lunch. I only saw it in the planning stages, so I'm excited."

"I hope that works out," Val said. "Be sure and tell the girls if you end up going. They were there on a field trip in May."

"I'll keep that in mind. Anyway, see you both over there. Are you going together?"

Oh. Logistically possible. They could put all three girls in the back seat of his truck. Except they never had and likely never would.

She threw out the first explanation that came to her. "It's better if I pick up the girls and meet Teague over there. He likes arriving ahead of time in case he and Zeke have any prep to do before the lesson."

"I can understand that. By the way, that's a jaunty look, wearing a bandana around your neck."

"I like it. Makes me feel more like a cowgirl."

"And way better than makeup, which you might sweat off." Laughter danced in her eyes. "Can't wait to see the lesson!" She hurried out of the barn.

Val put her hands to her hot cheeks. "This is ridiculous. Why am I blushing?"

Teague smiled. "I'm not sure. This morning you said it was no big deal."

"It isn't! When I was a teenager, I was embarrassed by a hickey, but I'm almost thirty years old, for God's sake. What's up with this silly blush?"

"Technically I should be the one who's blushing. I'm the responsible party, not you."

"You're exactly right, but you're cool as a cucumber."

"My mom's suffered through so many awkward moments with me that I guess we're both bullet-proof by now. She's not shocked and I'm not embarrassed."

"I should have guessed she'd know why I'm suddenly wearing the bandana." She groaned. "And if she did, then Ed probably—"

"Wouldn't be surprised."

"But I doubt the girls will."

"Sure hope not. Now if *they* started teasing me about it, I for sure would blush."

"I think you're safe. But Nell and Zeke might."

"I can handle those two. Oh, and good recovery on the transportation issue."

"Thanks. I had to think fast."

"Smart lady." He gazed at her. "I'm sure you've figured out we have some private time on our hands." He tilted his head toward the back of the barn.

"I have." And her reaction would surprise him. It sure as heck surprised her.

"It's about time to check the tack and see if any of it needs repairing. Care to help me? If we leave the barn door open, we'll hear Ed's truck and know when the coast is clear."

She took a deep breath. "I can't believe I'm saying this, but I... want a rain check."

Disappointment flickered in his eyes for a split second and was gone, replaced by a look of mild curiosity. "Not quite so vulnerable to straw, after all?"

More than ever, so why was she so reluctant to follow through? "I think it's all the talk about the girls and knowing I'll be picking them up and trying to act normal, when I'm..." She glanced at him. "When they leave, I'd like to go home."

His eyes widened. "Permanently? While my mom's still—"

"No, no, not permanently. I wouldn't do that to you."

His shoulders dropped with relief. "Scared me for a second."

"Sorry. I should have said it differently. I'd like to drive home, get cleaned up in my own shower, fetch the mail out of the mailbox."

"I hadn't thought about your mail."

"Honestly, I hadn't either until this chance opened up. If I empty the mailbox today, it'll be fine until Sunday. While I'm there, I might as well gather up what I need to take to school on Friday."

"Guess so."

"I could pick it up on the trip in Friday morning, but this way I don't have to think about it."

So logical. So not in keeping with her mood this morning.

"It's not about the mail and the school supplies, is it?"

She met his gaze. A hint of sadness lingered there. "Not exactly. I feel the need to reconnect with my little house before I pick up the girls."

"All right."

"I'll feel more like my old self if I do that. I can block out—" She cringed. "That sounded awful. I didn't mean—"

"It's okay. You said that living with me would be a stretch. You've done great so far. Makes sense that you need a break."

"You've done great, too." She moved closer. "Really super. I've had a terrific time."

He leaned the pitchfork against the side of the stall and wrapped her in a loose, undemanding hug. "So have I. Thank you."

"You're welcome. So far it's been… informative." Ugh. "That was the wrong word, too. Like this has been a research project."

"Well, you are a teacher."

She gazed up at him. Such kind eyes. She wanted to kiss him. Did she dare? That floaty feeling was back. "While you check on the tack, I'll head to the house and gather up my laundry."

"I don't have to check the tack." Understanding registered in his expression. "But I'm sure I can find something to do."

Her chest tightened. Standing on tiptoe, she gave him a fast kiss and eased out of his loose embrace. "See you at the lesson."

23

Shortly after two-thirty, Teague made the turn onto the dirt road leading to the Buckskin. He'd chosen not to read too much into Val's decision. Clearly it was the right one for her and possibly the right one for him, too.

He'd soon be dealing with those four perceptive little munchkins. The emotions from an intense lovemaking session at noon might still be rolling through his system at three.

But he'd missed her when he'd gone back to the house to make lunch and get cleaned up for the lesson. He'd wanted her to be sitting at the kitchen table while they had sandwiches and chips. Stepping into the shower to find her shampoo and conditioner gone had made his chest hurt.

He longed to have her sitting in the passenger seat next to him with those cute little girls in the back, chattering away. And if he missed her that much now, when she'd only created a break of a few hours, what would it be like when....

Oh, yeah, he was royally screwed.

Nobody else had arrived when he parked his truck in front of the barn. Good. He needed a moment to haul himself out of his funk before it was show time.

When he walked into the barn, Zeke was whistling some peppy little song as he used a push broom on some straw left in the aisle. Wasn't he a happy bastard?

He glanced up and grinned. "How's the engagement going?"

"Don't ask."

"Too late. But you can tell me to mind my own business."

"Mind your own business." He ducked into the tack room to fetch his rope, plus Claire's. He came out to find Zeke leaning against Lucky's stall, arms crossed. "Lying in wait, Zeke?"

"Leaning in wait is more accurate. If you tell me one more time to mind my own business and put some oomph into it, I'll go back to my broom."

Teague sighed and rubbed the back of his neck where tension was slowly working its way up to his skull. "About ten minutes ago, I figured out I'm so deep in caca I can't see over the top."

"Ahhh, dude. Sounds bad. Are you sure?"

"I'd love to be wrong, but I don't think I am."

"We all have such great hopes. Well, except Nell. She still insists this is a runaway train."

"She's probably right. Val's even more paranoid about getting into a serious relationship than I realized. Last night I thought I saw a glimmer of light in the tunnel, but—"

"It was the damn train coming at you?"

"Yessir. We're not even halfway through this, and today around eleven she felt the need to go back to her house for a couple of hours and regroup."

"Did you do something to set her off?"

"Don't think so. We had some unexpected time alone at the ranch when Ed and my mom went to Henri's for lunch, which meant we could.... you know."

"Sure do."

"But she took advantage of the opportunity to go home and check the mail."

"Ouch."

"I kind of get her reasoning. She's picking up the girls today like normal, and having sex with me an hour or so before she did that might make her feel uncomfortable with those kids."

"And they're famous for picking up on stuff."

"But it's not just her decision to cool it that bugs me. I told myself not to overthink her decision to leave, but it's almost like she was... hell, not almost, she *absolutely* was eager to get away from me."

"Hmm." Zeke stroked his chin.

"That's hard to admit. I mean, last night she was really — not to brag — but she wanted me bad. This morning, too, but we didn't have time. Yet then she takes off like a scared rabbit."

"You just hit the nail on the head, buddy. She's scared."

"I understand that. She doesn't want to get trapped in a bad marriage. And I've promised to cut out any kind of romantic gesture while she's staying with me, except when my mom's around. I swear I've stuck to that pledge."

"She's scared of more than getting trapped in a bad marriage. She's scared of falling in *love* with *you*." He jabbed a finger at Teague to emphasize his point.

"No." His breath hitched. "Yeah, she craves my body, but like I said, I'm not trying to woo her at all. It's strictly physical between us."

"I'm not saying she's head-over-boots. Not yet. But if she feels it coming on and she's starting to lose control, she might panic and run like the wind."

"Huh." He stared at the scarred floorboards. Was it possible? Looking up at Zeke, he shook his head. "Nope, can't buy it. I wish you were right, but I don't think so."

"It's just a theory." He shrugged. "I could be wrong. Anyway, she's not bailing on the engagement thing, is she?"

"She promised she wouldn't do that."

"Then you have a little more room. You can watch for signs. Running away doesn't always mean what you think it does."

"That's the other thing. After she left, I missed her like the devil. I'm confused about what's going on with her, but me? No confusion whatsoever. I'm in—"

"Dad! Uncle Teague!" Claire raced into the barn, her blond braid flying out behind her. "Auntie Ed's here!" She gave a little jump of joy. "And Gramma Henri! And Auntie Madeline!" More hopping. "It'll be like a *dress rehearsal* for Saturday!"

Teague smiled. His mom had been added to the pack.

"That's great, sweetheart." Zeke rested his hands on her shoulders, gently holding her still. "But let's remember our barn manners. You don't want to get Lucky agitated."

She grinned. "You're so funny, Daddy. Nothing agitates Lucky. He's the calmest horse in the world. But Thunder's another story. And Mister Rogers and Cinnamon are new here. I'll take it easy."

"Thank you."

"But isn't this perfect? I'm so glad Riley brought Mister Rogers over this morning instead of waiting until Saturday. We'll all be mounted up. But where is everybody gonna sit?"

"Who?"

"The audience."

"Those three ladies will be good with the fence," Teague said. "But we'll need something better for Saturday. Why don't you ask Auntie Ed if she'll loan out a section of her bleachers?"

Claire's eyes grew wide. "But they're *huge*." She spread out her arms. "How would we get them over here?"

"They come apart and a couple of pickups can bring them over. Talk to Uncle Matt and Uncle Jake. The Brotherhood could handle it, no problem."

"Yes, sir!" She snapped him a salute. "Could I please have my rope?"

"Oh, right." He took it off his shoulder and handed it to her. "Forgot I had it."

"Thanks!" She zipped out again.

Zeke laughed. "Sending a little girl to do a man's job?"

"You bet I am. When Claire asks, Claire gets. You're the only person who can tell her no."

"Me and Nell."

"Because she thinks of Nell as her mom?"

"She pretty much does, and we're thrilled about that, but Nell was her teacher before she stepped into the mom role. When Nell puts on her no-nonsense teacher face, Claire does exactly as she's told. It's magic."

"I've seen that no-nonsense teacher face."

"On Val?"

"Well, yeah. But I also grew up with it."

"So you did."

"But you're right, Val has that expression down pat, too." He sighed. "She'd make a great mom."

"You said that in your discouraged voice. Like you're halfway to giving up."

"I'm not, but I need to be somewhat realistic so I won't be destroyed if she dumps me on Sunday night."

Zeke nudged back his hat and gazed at him. "Is that a possibility?"

"That she'll dump me? She's been saying that's exactly what's going to happen. She says it's for my own good so I can find a woman who wants to get married."

"That's effed up."

"I know, but she believes it."

"Too bad. That wasn't what I was asking about, though. I was referring to the part about you being destroyed if she dumps you. Would you be?"

"I hope not."

"I hope not, too. I'd hate to lose you."

"That's nice to hear."

"At least not before you've taught me those nifty rope tricks." Zeke clapped him on the shoulder. "Enough chit-chat. We need to move our—"

"Dad, look!" Claire dashed back in. "Miss Jenson brought me *this*." She struck a pose and pointed to the purple bandana tied around her neck.

Teague swallowed a laugh. "Looks great, Claire."

"I know. Purple is my color. Riley's got a red one, Piper's is green and Tatum's is blue. They match our ropes. How cool is that?"

"Very cool." Zeke nodded. "How did Miss Jenson come up with that?"

"She decided to wear one today, so she brought bandanas for each of us, even Nell and you guys."

Teague damn near choked to death to keep from cracking up. He didn't dare look at Zeke.

"For us, too?" Zeke cleared his throat. "What color did we get?"

"Since the adults don't have colored ropes, Miss Jenson matched yours to your water bottles."

"I see. So mine is—"

"Pink."

Teague coughed into his hand to cover the snort that escaped despite his efforts. At the beginning of the summer, Nell had gifted everyone with a water bottle, each a different color to personalize them for reuse. Zeke had ended up with bright pink.

"And you'd better think about that when you pick a shirt to wear on Saturday."

Zeke's voice sounded a little strangled. "We're wearing the bandanas on Saturday?"

"Well, duh. That's the whole idea. They'll add pizazz! Just don't wear that brown and orange plaid one. Black would be good."

"I agree."

"So, are you guys all done in here, then?" Claire backed toward the door. "Because I think it's time to get this show on the road."

"We're on our way, sweetheart."

"Great! See you outside." She took off.

Teague started for the door.

"Hang on, lover boy." Zeke grabbed his shoulder. "Was it the hickey that got you in the doghouse?"

"No, it was not." He turned back and flashed Zeke a grin. "She said they were souvenirs of what a great time we had last night."

"Souvenirs, as in multiple ones? You were a busy boy."

"Just two, smartass."

"I know at least one was on her neck. Where was—"

"You'll never know." He walked out of the barn and tugged down the brim of his hat to block the sunlight.

The four girls stood in their usual practice area twirling their ropes. Today they looked more like a unit than they had all summer, partly because they'd finally learned to synchronize their routine.

But Val's solution to her dilemma had produced an unexpected consequence. Matching ropes and bandanas had transformed a random group of kids twirling ropes into a color-coordinated team.

Val stood talking with Nell, Ed, Henri and his mother. She clutched two bandanas, Zeke's bright pink one and a silver-gray for him.

Clearly she'd added a shopping trip to her rounds. Good thing the tourist season wasn't over and the shops still carried novelties like this. She'd scored a yellow one for Nell and an orange one for herself.

She glanced in his direction and he gave her a subtle thumbs-up. She sent him a wink in return.

Although they'd been apart less than four hours, he was hungry for the sight of her. He stood, mesmerized, until a nudge from Zeke snapped him out of it.

"Here's a tip, buddy," Zeke murmured. "Don't stare at her like a forlorn puppy. You don't win points that way."

"Have you been talking to Riley?"

"About what?"

"Her dog."

"She has a dog?"

"Yes, and—"

"What's her dog got to do with you making goo-goo eyes at Val?"

"A lot. I'll explain some other time. After I show off my nifty rope tricks. You're welcome to watch and learn."

"I will, right after I fetch my pink bandana."

"Sorry about that."

"Oh, no, don't apologize. It takes a manly man to pull off pink, especially worn as a bandana around my manly neck."

"I owe you one."

"Yes, you do. I'm torn between a drink and a saddle covered in bling. I'm leaning toward the saddle."

"I'd lean toward the drink if I were you. The saddle could take a while."

"No worries. Living with Nell has taught me to be a patient man. A manly, patient man." He squeezed Teague's shoulder. "Watch and learn, buddy. Watch and learn."

24

The bandanas earned Val an unmerciful amount of subtle teasing from the adults. Teague got his share, too. All the jokes went right over the heads of those little girls, though. They adored the concept, as Val had guessed they would.

Claire's labeling of the lesson as a dress rehearsal had turned out to be prophetic. Like most dress rehearsals, the lesson had soldiered through glitch after glitch.

Adding Cinnamon and Mister Rogers to the mix had caused Butch and Sundance to act up. Butch was so rambunctious that Nell had fallen off. Only her pride was hurt, fortunately.

The girls had tangled ropes during their demonstration and they hadn't done that since the second or third week of roping lessons. Teague had loused up one of his elaborate tricks. He never did that.

But their three spectators had raved about the performance. Madeline fit right in with the other two aunties and she'd been an immediate hit with the kids. At the end of the lesson, when everyone gathered in front of the barn to finish off their water, Val had mentioned that Madeline was coming along for the classroom project the next day. The girls had all cheered.

Teague's bobbled rope trick was no surprise. He'd clearly been distracted during the event. She had been, too. It was a wonder Nell had taken a tumble and not her. She hadn't brought her A-game to the lesson.

Evidently she'd brought her teenage self, though. She was crushing on the guy. When he'd walked out of the barn, his cute thumbs-up gesture had made her giddy. Her sly wink might have looked cool and sophisticated, but it hadn't matched her racing pulse.

She'd looked for an excuse, any excuse to go talk to him. The bandana had been the obvious ploy. But Madeline had drawn her into a conversation about Raptors Rise and she hadn't been able to find a polite way to excuse herself.

He'd stood there looking at her for quite a while, as if deep in thought. Her brain had regressed to that of a sixteen-year-old. Was he thinking about their time apart? Had it seemed like forever to him, too?

Eventually he'd come over to collect his bandana. Their fingers had brushed. They'd made brief eye contact. Too short. She'd wanted more. Then they'd both been swept up in the chaos.

But they'd come to the end of the lesson, thank goodness. She was impatient to end the chatter and take the girls home. Maybe she and Teague would have a little alone time before they walked up to Ed's for dinner. Yep, she'd developed an inconvenient crush. All the signs were there.

The hours apart had revealed it. Instead of relief at being back in her own space, she'd dealt with restless energy. The house that had been her refuge held no interest for her because Teague wasn't there.

Okay, so she had a crush. She'd experienced those before and they always faded. Sooner or later the guy said or did something that burst the bubble and she was over him. Teague would be no different.

Separation wasn't the answer, though. The old saying *absence makes the heart grow fonder* was right on the money. She needed to get back to that twenty-four-hour connection. That was her best chance to break the spell.

When was this gathering going to break up, for crying out loud? Guess it was up to her. "Well, girls, time to get going. I don't want your parents to start worrying."

Riley, Piper and Tatum gave her matching looks of unhappy resignation. They adored being here.

"Just remember, we'll be back Saturday."

"But then it's *over*." Riley's entire body slumped as only a limber child could slump and still remain upright. "I *hate* that."

"Why does it have to be over?" Ed glanced at Teague and Zeke. "Why couldn't you keep this up on Saturdays, even after school starts?"

Claire leaped on the idea. "Daddy, could we? Could we *please*?"

Zeke glanced at Henri. "It's not my decision."

"If it's mine, then I say go for it." Henri turned to Ed. "Assuming you're going with that Cinnamon plan we discussed."

"I am. Claire, it's time for Cinnamon to be stabled over here, where you can interact with him every day."

"*Really*?" Claire's eyes grew enormous and she began to quiver. "You mean it?"

"I never say something that important if I don't mean it."

Claire whispered a soft *wow* and gulped. "I don't... I can't..." She raced to Ed, grabbed her around the waist and hugged her so tight that Ed began to gasp.

"Sweetheart." Zeke stepped forward and gently pried her away. "Auntie Ed can't breathe."

"Sorry, Auntie Ed." Claire glanced up, her face wet. She sniffed. "I kinda lost it."

"That's okay, sweetie." Ed didn't sound totally steady, either. "And just so you know, I'm not giving him to you. If I did that, you and your daddy would end up paying for vet bills and shoeing and all the other stuff."

Zeke kept his hand on Claire's shoulder as he faced Ed. "I would gladly do that."

"I know you would, but you don't need to worry about it just yet. We'll see how it goes."

"I might need to leave Mister Rogers here, too," Riley said. "My folks are thinking of moving into town. And my mom just read that a horse is happier around other horses. They said they'd be happy to pay rent if he can stay here."

"He can certainly stay," Henri said. "And your mom is right. Horses are herd animals. They get lonely."

"Riley, if your folks agree, you can ride home with Claire and me a couple times a week."

"That would be awesome, Miss O'Connor. That way I won't miss him so much."

"Well, then." Ed looked around, focusing on each of the participants. "Is everybody in?"

"I have to check with my mom and dad," Tatum said. "But I'll bet they say yes."

Piper nodded. "Me, too, but they think this is great for me, so they'll probably say yes."

Piper and Tatum were the only ones who couldn't commit on the spot. The rest, including Teague, were enthusiastically for it.

Ed turned to Val, eyebrows raised. The woman was no fool. She understood continuing the lessons would mean an ongoing connection with Teague.

No pressure. Val cleared her throat. "I should probably think about this. I'm not sure I—"

"Oh, Miss Jenson, you have to do it!" Claire started off the pleading.

"Yes, you have to!" Riley piled on. "It wouldn't be the same without you."

"That's for sure." Piper shoved her glasses back in place. "Especially since you'll see us every day at school and if you don't do it, you'll be sad."

"And we'll be *very* sad. We'll look like this." Tatum pulled down the corners of her mouth, her gaze comically woeful.

Ah, those girls. It wasn't in her best interests. She was stepping right back into the cow patty she'd lived through all summer. But four adorable munchkins had her by the heartstrings. "Okay. I'll do it."

The girls whooped, hollered and ran over to hug her the way Claire had hugged Ed. Anyone would think she'd just given them a trophy.

Surrounded by jubilant girls, she looked over their heads to find Teague watching the action with a soft smile. God, he was handsome. Her stomach fluttered with awareness. Who wouldn't be infatuated with a man like him?

She had three more nights to work through it. Time to get started on that program. "Hey, guys." She eased away from their enthusiastic hugs. "Now we really need to go. You don't want to be late for dinner when you're planning to ask for a favor."

"Yes, ma'am." Piper, the most mature of the four, broke away first. "Riley, Tatum, got your ropes?"

They both held them up.

"Then let's move out."

"I'll walk you over there." Claire fell into step with them.

"I'm right behind you, ladies." Val handed her water bottle to Nell. "'Bye, everyone." She was several yards away when Teague hailed her.

His long strides closed the distance quickly. "Need to tell you something."

"What?"

He lowered his voice. "Mom mentioned this earlier but there was never a good time to tell you. She and Ed are joining the Babes for their monthly sleepover at Henri's tonight."

"We're not having dinner with them?"

"Right. They're staying here until sometime tomorrow morning."

"Oh." They'd have the ranch to themselves. That would be fun.

"I wanted you to know in case..." He dropped his voice even lower. "In case you want to go back to your house tonight, take an even longer break from me before we head into the homestretch. My mom will never know."

The homestretch. Interesting choice of words. "I appreciate the thought."

"Okay, then. If you show up around dawn to help me feed, that should be good enough. Those ladies usually sleep in after their big night, so I don't expect Mom and Ed back before—"

"I'd rather stay with you."

His eyes widened. Then his face lit up. "You would?"

"Yes."

"Hot damn."

25

After Val drove away, Teague excused himself from the group gathered in front of the barn and climbed in his truck. He had things to do.

The old Teague would have stopped in town for candles, flowers, and a sinfully rich dessert. He would have cooked a complicated meal and laid chocolates on the pillow. But that was before he'd learned a thing or two about Valerie Rose Jenson.

Instead he bought a couple of T-bones, potatoes and a can of ranch beans. Dessert would be chocolate chip cookies from the market's bakery.

He assessed the weather as he drove home. A few clouds hung over the mountains. A nice sunset would be a bonus, but it wouldn't make or break the plan.

He'd probably have the horses rounded up and fed by the time Val got back, but if not, no matter. This wasn't a set-the-scene kind of night. More a choose-your-own-adventure.

Driving straight to the barn, he parked the truck, fetched lead ropes and brought Silver and

Nugget in from the pasture. They'd eat first so they'd be finished by the time he needed them.

Then he gathered the rest of the small herd, permanently down by one more. He'd miss Cinnamon, but Ed was doing the right thing. Grooming Claire to be a champion meant strengthening the bond between that girl and her barrel-racing horse. Claire and Cinnamon would be stars if Ed had anything to do with it.

Everyone was munching away as he hopped in the truck and drove back to the house. Val was just pulling in. The sight of her little truck got his blood pumping.

She was going to love this evening. As would he. If she ditched him on Sunday, he'd have this night to console him. Making love in the barn on a bed of straw was a nice fantasy, but it lacked range. He was going for an indelible memory.

He parked next to her truck, grabbed the bag of groceries from the passenger seat and climbed out. "Fancy meeting you here."

She smiled. "I was thinking the same thing. What's in the bag?"

"Dinner."

"Take-out?"

"No, ma'am. We're cooking."

"As I recall, that got complicated on Tuesday night." She started up the porch steps.

"This won't. We're taking the horses and going for a cowboy cookout."

She spun around to face him. "Teague, I love that idea!"

He grinned. "Knew you would."

"What can I do?"

"Not much. After I pick up a few things in the house, you can help me carry everything down to the barn and pack it into saddlebags."

"I'm *so* excited." She hurried across the porch and went inside. "We're building a campfire and everything?"

He laughed as he followed her in. "You didn't get to go camping as a kid, did you?"

"No! My parents were phobic about the great outdoors. I was *dying* to go into the woods, build a fire and cook food. It wasn't in the cards."

"Now it is."

"What are we taking?"

The light in her eyes made him smile. "Most of it's in the kitchen. In the bottom left cupboard there's a kit that has all the utensils and cookware we'll need."

"I'm on it." She darn near skipped into the kitchen. "This?" She pulled out the kit. "It's not very big."

"It's compact on purpose." He set the groceries on the counter and took a canvas bag out of a drawer. "You'll see it has everything when we unpack it."

"All right. What else?"

"Aluminum foil. Just tear off enough to wrap two potatoes. The oven mitts. Tongs." He quickly transferred the food to the canvas bag. "We need to get a move on so we're at the meadow before dark. It's easier to gather firewood when it's still light."

"Firewood? We're not using briquettes?"

"Briquettes are for amateurs."

"Ah, Teague, you sure know the way to a woman's heart."

He didn't, not for sure, but he was giving it his best shot.

Ten minutes later, they walked down to the barn carrying their supplies. He'd tucked a rolled quilt under one arm. The hatchet and his rope were in the tack room.

"I don't have to ask you what the quilt is for."

"Sitting on."

"Uh-huh. Did you bring—"

"I did. In my pocket. But just to be clear, we're cooking and eating first. If you fool around and neglect to collect firewood and build a fire before it gets dark, all you'll have is a romp in a very dark wooded area. That's not a cowboy cookout."

"I want the whole shebang."

"I figured. That's why I brought my harmonica."

"You play the harmonica? How did I miss that?"

"I don't take it out for just anybody."

"Ha, ha. Are you any good?"

"Which instrument are we talking about?"

"Your harmonica. I've experienced your skill with the other one."

"I'm slightly better with the harmonica."

"Whoa. Then you belong on the stage in Nashville."

"Golly gosh. Thank you, ma'am." That earned him a grin. What an idiot he'd been. She'd come right out and said she'd chosen Montana because it was full of cowboys. He'd had that ace in the hole all this time and hadn't played it.

"Do you want me to tack up the horses or pack the saddle bags?"

"Tack up Nugget, please, while I pack the bags. Then you can hang around and admire my bulging muscles while I tack up Silver, who's a slow eater."

She sighed. "I've created an egocentric monster. Note to self. Eliminate all complimentary references to Teague's muscles. Ditto his package."

"Ever hear of closing the barn door after the horse escapes?"

"Are you saying your swelled head is a permanent condition?"

"Could be. When I'm around you, everything swells."

"Hey, cut it out. You said we had to make the campfire first thing."

"We do. To quote a dear friend of mine, I'm just priming the pump."

"Sounds vaguely familiar."

"Great phrase. Stuck with me." He waited for her to go through the open door and then followed. Her priming-the-pump comment this morning hadn't meshed with her raincheck move a few hours later. Now she was trading sexy banter again.

Why was she blowing hot and cold? Was Zeke right? Could she be falling for him and had no clue how to handle it? Maybe so. Given her fear of getting trapped in a terrible marriage, falling in love would be the last thing she'd want.

While she went to fetch Nugget, he stepped into the tack room and pulled two sets of saddlebags from the top shelf. Had to dust them off.

They hadn't had much use since Ed had cut back to one wrangler. Prior to that he and the other hands had made a weekly thing of cowboy cookouts. Sort of like the Buckskin Brotherhood gatherings around the fire pit behind the bunkhouse.

He hadn't been out to this meadow in — geez — a couple of years? What if the fire pit stones had been scattered? The fire pit was near Crooked Creek, the same one that ran through Buckskin land. It could have flooded that meadow since the last time he'd ridden out that way.

Too late to do anything about it, now. He began loading the bags.

"Those look way cool."

He glanced up. Val had come in for Nugget's tack. "They are way cool."

"Love the fringe. I've seen things like that in the movies."

"You might've seen these very saddlebags in the movies. Originally they were props, likely handled by some of the big stars. Ed was in the right place at the right time when the studio put them up for sale."

"They look like they should be in a museum." She hung Nugget's bridle on the saddle and picked it up, along with the blanket and pad.

"Ed's not much for putting good equipment in a museum." He tucked the wrapped T-bones in carefully. "I'm glad we're doing this.

Tomorrow morning I'll give these some oil and get the tarnish off the silver."

She paused in the doorway. "Can I help?"

"Aren't you and my mom going into town to work on your classroom?"

"Oh, right."

"Want me to hold off until you come back?"

"No, that's okay. You probably want to get it—"

"I'll wait."

She smiled. "Thanks." She left, looking for all the world like a seasoned cowgirl as she handled that tack. Whether she was here or at the Buckskin, she'd taken to ranch life as if she'd been born to it.

Not to make excuses for himself, but his proposal in June hadn't come out of nowhere. His house, this ranch, hell, even *he* fit her like a glove. He'd cut to the chase for a reason. When something was perfect, why waste time?

<u>26</u>

The trail, wide enough for two horses, looked familiar. Val glanced over at Teague. "Is this the same one we went on before?"

"Yes, ma'am." He nudged Silver into a trot. "Thought we'd take it a little faster this time since we're going about three times as far."

"Fine with me." She settled in, matching her motion to the horse's strides. "I thought Nugget had a rough trot. Turns out the roughness was all on my side."

"You've come a long way."

"It's been fun. I was so afraid I'd be bad at this."

"Instead you have a natural talent for it."

"Who knew?"

"Ready to kick it up a notch?"

"You bet."

He made a clucking sound with his tongue and Silver surged forward into a canter.

Nugget followed Silver's lead, skimming along the ground, his white mane rippling in the breeze, his golden coat glowing in the last rays of the setting sun. His hoofbeats matched Silver's cadence, as if they were dancing.

Beside her, Teague rode with a fluid grace she had yet to achieve, a broad-shouldered hero on a white horse. He looked over and smiled.

As if a shutter clicked, her heart captured the beautiful moment. No matter what happened between her and Teague, she'd have this precious memory. She'd be forever grateful for that.

He faced forward again. "Better slow it down as we head into the trees." He eased back on the reins and brought Silver down to a trot and then a walk.

"It's amazing how different this ride feels from the one back in June. I thought we went quite far, but we didn't even make it to the trees."

"We walked them most of the way. You don't get far when you amble along. We only trotted a little bit."

She laughed. "Because it hurt like hell!"

"I seem to remember you complaining a lot."

"I seem to remember you soothing me after we got back with some well-placed kisses."

His teeth flashed. "Think you'll need more soothing after this ride?"

"Count on it."

"Greenhorns. Gotta love 'em."

She surveyed the trail ahead. Trees and more trees. "Are we there yet?"

He chuckled. "No."

"Can you ride and play your harmonica at the same time?"

"Sure, as long as we're walking them. Silver knows the way."

"It would be very atmospheric if you played your harmonica while we saunter along. It would be like a singing cowboy movie."

"Minus the singing."

"If I know the song, I'll sing."

"Do you know Red River Valley?"

"I do! I teach it to my kids every year. It's a fascinating song."

"Because it's about a woman who's breaking a cowboy's heart to bits?"

"Oh, but it's not that simple. There's another version in which it's a girl whose heart is breaking to bits."

"But it's sung by a cowboy who doesn't want a woman to leave."

"In the most current one, yes, but the song's been around a long time. There's lots of info and scholarly debate connected to *Red River Valley*."

"But either way, someone's leaving someone else."

"Maybe not by choice, though. It could be circumstances. We can't assume the intention is to break someone's heart to bits."

"I suppose not." Looping the reins around the saddle horn, he unsnapped his shirt pocket, pulled out a shiny silver harmonica and tapped it on his palm. "In any case, I'm just playing the tune. The words are your job. Ready?"

"Yes, I am. I'll count you in."

His eyebrows lifted. "Oh, will you, now?"

"I handle the music program at Apple Grove Elementary."

"I see. This is more serious business than I thought. Let me warm up first." Moistening his lips, he brought the harmonica to his mouth and played a quick scale.

Mm. His supple mouthing of the harmonica sent little arrows of awareness straight to her...

"You said you'd count me in?"

"Sorry. Got distracted by a bird in the trees."

"What bird?"

"Never mind. On three. One, two, *three*." She gestured to him.

The sweet notes that came out of that harmonica took her breath away.

He stopped playing. "Weren't you going to sing?"

"Yes! That crazy bird again. Let's start over." She faced forward, away from his tempting self. "One, two, *three*." She managed to sing the opening without making a complete fool of herself.

By the time she reached the chorus, her vocal cords were limbered up and her delivery improved. Then she was into it, letting the music flow through her. She was darned proud of how she finished up, holding the note almost as long as he did.

"Beautiful voice."

She turned to look at him, adrenaline making her heart race. "Thanks. Beautiful job on the harmonica. Loved the vibrato at the end."

His gaze held hers. "Thank you. I had no idea you could sing like that."

"In normal life, people don't usually burst into song like they do in musical theater."

"Were you in musical theater?"

"In high school and college, but it wasn't the career for me."

"Why not?"

"It's very tough to make a living on a consistent basis. I loved performing, but not enough to give my whole life to what could turn out to be a vagabond existence. Teaching elementary-age kids in this great little town is my dream job."

He tucked the harmonica back in his pocket and picked up the reins. "I'm stunned that I've spent all this time with you and didn't know about your singing."

"Like I said, why would you?"

"Does anybody know?"

"My principal, Harland Kuhn. It was on my application, which is one of the reasons he hired me. He needed someone to handle the music program. They don't have the budget to hire a music teacher."

"Well, I'm really glad I brought the harmonica."

"So am I. But I'm curious. What made you think of it?"

"A few years ago, one of the hands found out I played and talked me into taking my harmonica when we'd come out for our weekly cookout."

"Now when do you play?"

"Sometimes while I'm sitting on the porch in the evening."

"With nobody around to appreciate it?"

"There's me. I like it."

"Well, there you go. That's something I completely understand, doing something for its own sake because it makes you happy. Even if nobody else is involved."

"Do you sing in your house when you're all by yourself?"

"Now that you mention it." She stared at the trail ahead. She didn't admit that to most people. To any people, to be precise. "It's one of the perks of living alone. I don't have to consider whether it would bother anybody."

"It wouldn't bother me if you sang while I'm around. I'd like it."

"I'd like it if you'd play your harmonica when I'm around. You sound great."

"I will if you will."

"It's a deal." She smiled. Would they follow through? Maybe not, but the possibility intrigued her. "Hey, are we there yet?"

"About two more minutes."

"How will I know?"

"First you'll hear the water. Then the trail dead-ends at the meadow. You can't go on without crossing the creek."

"Is the water cold?"

"Very. It's fed by snow melt."

"I take it you've been in it?"

"Plenty of times, but always in the middle of the day when it's hot. At night, it's a great ice chest. We'll stick a couple of bottles of apple cider in there to keep them cold."

"I've always wanted to wade in a mountain creek. This is my chance."

"If you fall in, your clothes will get wet."

"I won't fall in."

"The rocks are slippery."

"I'll be careful. Do you want to?"

"Not this time of day. I don't relish—"

"But we're building a fire. You can dry your clothes by the fire."

"A shirt, maybe. But jeans? Only if you keep the fire going all night. Even then the seams will still be damp."

"Then I'll roll mine up and be super careful. I hear the water! Tell you what, I'll get my creek wading in first thing. Get it out of the way. Cross it off my list."

"If you fall in, I'm not coming after you. You'll have to get yourself out."

"I won't fall in."

27

Val fell in. Teague had seen it coming, but she'd been one determined lady.

She'd started her adventure after helping him hobble the horses and turn them out to graze. Together they'd spread out the quilt and laid the saddlebags on it.

He was supposed to be unpacking while she went wading, but he'd delayed while he'd kept his eye on her noisy progress into the water. She'd squealed at the icy temperature but she'd kept going. She'd wobbled once and regained her balance.

He'd fetched his rope.

She'd fallen on her tush in the middle of the creek. Every effort to right herself ended with her falling again, swearing a blue streak and heaping blame on herself for being stupid.

"You're not stupid." He uncoiled the rope as he approached the muddy bank of the creek. "Just inexperienced."

"But you *told* me this was a bad idea. Did I listen? No, I knew better! And now I'm freezing my ass off, and my jeans won't dry unless we keep the fire going all night, and we haven't gathered firewood yet, and—"

"I'm going to toss you a loop. Tighten it around your waist. Then I'll pull you out."

"It's more than I deserve."

He ducked his head to hide a grin. Then he cleared his throat. "Want me to leave you there? I could put your steak on a plate and float it out to you."

"I'd probably dump the plate over and a carefully grilled T-bone would be carried away on the current. Toss me the rope, please."

Twirling the loop carefully, he judged the distance and sent it aloft. It settled down on the surface of the water, enclosing her perfectly. Bullseye.

"Teague, that was amazing!"

"Pick it up and tighten it around your waist before it gets too saturated to work right."

"Doing it." She followed his directions, as he gradually put more tension on the line. "Now what?"

"I'll plant myself here." He chose two large rocks and wedged his booted feet behind them. "Grab the rope in both hands. When it's taut, slowly stand up."

"Okay." She scooted around to face him and clutched the rope.

"That's good." Hand over hand, he took the slack out. "Almost ready. There. Stand up slowly. Keep holding on and I'll reel you in."

"Like a fish."

"A delectable fish."

"I can't believe I've screwed this up so royally."

"Not really. You can check this off your list. That's progress, right?"

"My jeans will never dry, just like you said."

"What a pity. You'll have to leave them off the rest of the night."

"So I'll ride home Lady Godiva style?"

"I can't have you doing that."

"You're right. Way too weird. I'll have to drag them on no matter how wet they are."

"Have you ever tried to ride a horse in soggy jeans? It's a miserable experience."

"I'm sure, but I'll just have to—"

"Here's an idea. How about if I drape you face-down across Nugget's saddle and lead you home like the lawmen used to bring in the desperados they'd gunned down?"

She started laughing. "Thanks, but I'll take the soggy jeans route."

"Aw, come on, Val. It'll be like performance art. We'll call it *Moon Over the Palomino*."

Her laughter turned to giggles. "You're horrible."

"How about *Ain't No Valley Low Enough, Ain't No Bottom High Enough*?"

"Stop it! I'm liable to dunk again."

"No, you won't." He pulled her the last two feet, reached out a hand and grabbed her. "I've got you." Dropping the end of the rope, he wrapped her in his arms, soaking the front of his jeans and shirt in the process. "I'm sorry you fell in."

"Aren't you going to say *I told you so*?"

"Not my style." Tilting her face up to his, he kissed her.

Big mistake. Once he started that, there was no stopping. She had to strip down, anyway, and his clothes weren't in much better shape. Might as well get naked and be done with it. He rescued a condom from his pocket while she moved the saddlebags to the grass. They tumbled to the quilt, laughing.

As he rolled the condom on, she gazed up at him. "This is exactly what you said we weren't supposed to do. Now we'll never find firewood."

"Yeah, we will. This is the modern age." Moving over her, he sought her heat. "We have flashlights." He drove deep.

She wrapped her arms around his back and her legs around his hips. "I'm sorry I ignored your advice."

"I'm not." He began to stroke.

Arching her back, she rose to meet his thrusts. "I'm not, either."

He loved her hard and fast. The shadowy woods and rushing water brought out the mountain man in him.

She didn't seem to mind. She responded with abandon, her cries blending with the slap of waves against rocks and the moan of the wind through the tops of the tall pines.

They climaxed together. He hadn't planned it, which made the sensation twice as glorious. He didn't want to move, didn't want to break the spell, but eventually the breeze on his sweaty back made him shiver.

She murmured something that sounded like *firewood.* Or maybe it was *higher good.* Bottom line, in a few minutes they'd be cold and hungry. Time to get with the original program.

Easing away from her, he walked naked to where he'd left the saddlebags beside the still-viable fire pit. He located a trash bag and disposed of the condom. Then he stood for a moment, chilly but energized.

"Whatcha doing?"

"Channeling my inner nudist. Too bad we can't just stay like this."

"I don't have much choice."

"You have some choice. I tucked a couple of nylon windbreakers in since they take up no space at all." He dug them out of a saddlebag before sitting on the blanket and handing one to her. "They lack feel-appeal, but they'll block the cold."

"Good thinking. But that only solves half the issue."

"My jeans are only wet in the front, so I can tolerate that while I fetch us some firewood."

"I'm not sure I could put mine on. And I really wanted to collect firewood, damn it."

"Tell you what. Wrap up in the quilt while I go look for a fallen branch with a lot of little ones still attached. I'll drag it over here and you can use the hatchet to break it up."

"I've never used a hatchet."

"Then I'll teach you how."

She gazed at him, her eyes luminous. "I know I'm the weakest link in this posse and I fell in the water which was a pain in the patoot for you, but I'm having the best time. I wish we had a tent so we could stay here."

"I wasn't planning to rush off after dinner."

"I mean for several days. Like pioneers in the wilderness."

"You really do want to go camping, don't you?"

"I really, really do! I didn't realize how much until you suggested going for a cookout. I thought I moved to Montana to be surrounded by cowboy culture. That's only part of the picture. I moved here for *all* of it."

"But Nell said you were reluctant to take riding lessons."

"Because what if I was bad at it? What if I'm not the least bit suited to this fantasy life I've carried around in my head since I was a little girl?"

"I think the evidence is mounting. After one summer of lessons, you're already a good hand. You don't shy away from any of it. You seem almost happy to muck out stalls with me. It's hot, sweaty work, yet you—what are you laughing about?"

"You don't get it, do you?"

"Get what?"

"It's not that I love shoveling horse poop, although I don't mind it. But I'm there for the moment when you strip off your T-shirt."

"You're kidding."

"Not kidding. If I had a video of you flexing those sweaty muscles as you muck out a stall, it would go viral in no time."

"Huh. Meaning you'd only be an eager stall mucker in the summertime?"

"Oh, I'd still be glad to do it regardless. There's a lot of satisfaction in making the barn nice for those sweet horses. But the prospect of seeing you shirtless and glistening is the major draw."

His groin tightened. "Too bad you'll be unavailable tomorrow morning. I hear it'll be unseasonably warm."

"I'll have to miss that opportunity." She reached over and stroked his chest. "But mucking out stalls isn't the only way to get those muscles sweaty."

His breath hitched. "If I follow up on that, we'll never build a fire."

"And I won't learn how to use a hatchet."

"That, too." He pushed himself to his feet.

"Do you think the pioneers had this problem?"

"Sure, although I wouldn't call it a problem." He glanced down at her, all tousled and rosy from lovemaking. "I'd call it a gift."

28

Riding home under a full moon capped off a night Val would never forget. She wasn't quite doing the Lady Godiva bit, but she wasn't fully clothed, either. Her panties had dried enough to put them on and she'd left her boots and socks on the bank, so they were fine.

The nylon windbreaker slithered against her arms and breasts when she moved, but it kept the top of her warmer than a damp shirt and bra would have. Teague had arranged the quilt over the saddle to make sure her bare legs weren't chafed. Nugget's warmth helped chase away the cold.

So did the memories she'd take back with her. Food cooked over a campfire had tasted amazing and making love under the stars had been magic. Afterward, she and Teague had settled back on the quilt, hands clasped, and listened to the sounds of the night.

The hoot of an owl, the yip of coyotes, the distant howl of a wolf — each had been wilder, closer, more thrilling in a mountain meadow rather than when they'd drifted through an open bedroom window. She wanted to do this again.

And there it was... her dilemma. Teague was her guide into this world. Yet she refused to take advantage of his generosity to continue an affair that wouldn't end the way he wanted. He'd played his part beautifully, keeping the tone light and the sex playful. That didn't mean he'd abandoned his dream of a wife and kids.

"How're you doing over there, pioneer lady?"

"Never better." She glanced over at him. "Silver almost glows in the moonlight."

"Night rides are his specialty. And indoor arenas. Ed and I like to keep him out of bright sun as much as possible. He's prone to sunburn."

"Yet he can jump through flaming hoops?"

"It's for a fraction of a second, not enough to affect him. He rarely does that these days, anyway. He's semi-retired, although put a trick saddle on him and he'll carry you around the arena while you're hanging upside down, your head inches from the arena floor."

"Have you tried it?"

"Yes, ma'am. Ed brought in a gymnastics coach and I trained for several months."

"Wow. Are you going to show me?"

"Afraid not. I'm out of practice. I decided it wasn't going to be a career path, and I gave up the training routine. Most of it, anyway. I still lift weights."

"Where? I haven't seen a weight bench." Just the results of that lifting. No wonder he was so ripped.

"Ed has a weight room I can use any time I want. She works out every day, one of the reasons she's still competing at almost eighty-six."

"Makes perfect sense. I should take a page out of her book. I wouldn't mind being that spry when I'm her age."

"She's always encouraging people to use her weight room if they show any interest at all. It's top-of-the-line equipment."

She didn't comment on the implied invitation. Starting an exercise routine connected with Ed's weight room would mean showing up at the ranch several times a week. Good for her muscles, not so good for creating distance between her and the man on the white horse.

"What time are you and my mom leaving tomorrow?"

"Nine-thirty. That'll give us time to pick up Tatum and Piper. Nell and Claire will swing by Riley's house and then meet as at the school by ten."

"You'll have fun."

"Big fun. So much has changed since last year. I met Nell for the first time while she was setting up her room. I knew we'd be friends after that first day, but I had no idea how she'd change my life. And Claire! Neither of us counted on that girl bursting onto the scene."

"Those four little devils sure did waylay you this afternoon."

"Yep."

"I'm glad they did. You need to keep riding, Val. After what you said tonight, I can't imagine you giving it up. That would be a step in the wrong direction."

"I know, but... it's complicated."

"By me. And that's not what I—"

"Not just you. I'm as much a part of this as you are. I could have turned you down flat on the fake engagement plan. I didn't." She turned to him. "And I don't regret saying yes. I wouldn't trade the past few days for anything."

"And nights. Don't leave out the nights."

"Believe me, I won't."

He took a deep breath. "I have to ask. Have you given any more thought to continuing—"

"Yes, and I always come to the same conclusion. If we're going to have any chance of salvaging a friendship out of this episode, we have to end our..." What to call it? "Our intimate relationship on Sun—"

"If you ask me, our *intimate relationship* has been a huge success."

"Which is all the more reason to quit while we're ahead. The obvious time is Sunday after your mom leaves."

He was quiet for a while. "You had a good time tonight."

"I had a *great* time tonight."

"There's a small window of opportunity left, before the first snow. It seems a shame to let that go to waste."

"You could invite—"

"Don't say it."

"But—"

"Val, I'm not going to turn around and take some other woman out there. Wouldn't be fair to her. All I'd think about would be the amazing time you and I had."

"Okay, I shouldn't have suggested you start dating someone else right away. That was insensitive."

"Come out to the meadow with me next weekend. If you don't wade in the creek, you'll get to help me collect firewood."

"We wouldn't need more. That pile we left was huge."

"So we should go use it up before it snows."

"You're not going to convince me, Teague. If we stop on Sunday, we'll end on a high note. We'll walk away smiling."

"Speak for yourself."

"I intend to end things amicably."

"*Amicably*. You know what? I hate that word. I picture two people with fake smiles pretending everything is just fine when it's not."

"You can have your definition and I'll have mine. I just agreed to continue riding lessons, and I want us to be able to enjoy being around each other during those lessons."

"I want that, too, which is why I think we should extend the time and ease into the eventual separation. When the weather cools off, we can start cooling off. I won't be stripping off my shirt to muck out stalls. That should help."

"Sarcasm doesn't become you."

"Sorry. This conversation is making me a little testy. What's so wrong about my idea? Why won't you at least try it for a few weeks?"

"Because I don't believe we'll cool off gradually. I think we'll dig a deeper hole for ourselves."

He didn't respond right away. When he did, his voice was much softer. "Because you'll fall in love with me?"

She sucked in a breath. *No!*

"That's it, isn't it? You're starting to fall for me and it scares you. You—"

"That's not it." Alarm bells jangled in her head. "I'll admit I have a crush on you, but—"

"Same thing."

Panic set in, elevating her heart rate, making her tremble. "It absolutely is *not* the same thing. A crush is a temporary infatuation. I figured out I was crushing on you when I went back to my house today and missed having you around."

"Aha! Because you're falling for me!"

She cleared her throat and reached for her rational teacher voice. "I understand why you'd want to believe that, but it's not true."

"Zeke thinks it is."

"Zeke's romance with Nell is coloring his judgment."

"He said you wanted to take a break from me today because you're scared that you're falling in love with me."

"Then why did I choose to stay with you tonight? If I'm so *scared*, I should have jumped at the chance to sleep in my own bed and gather my forces. Instead I'm out here cavorting with you."

"Arguing with me, you mean."

"*Now* I'm arguing. But earlier we were cavorting like crazy."

"Yes, we were, damn it, and it was wonderful. Why do you suppose that is, Val?"

"Because we like each other!"

"We sure as hell do. And we have *fun*. We've kept it light and breezy, just like I promised we would. I did it, Val, and I can keep doing it. Why do you want to end such a terrific experience? What are you afraid of?"

She gulped. "I'm not afraid."

"Are you sure about that?"

"Yes! I'm thinking about you, about what you want out of life."

"What if I said I don't care about that anymore?"

"I wouldn't believe you."

"That's too bad, because it's the truth. I'm ready to stop dreaming about some future that may or may not happen. I love what's happening in the present. And I think you're *nuts* to want to give it up."

"And I think *you're* ignoring your deep-seated longing for a family."

"No, I'm not."

"Yes, you are, Teague. I wish I had a video of your face when you proposed in June. You were positively *glowing* with excitement about marrying me. You couldn't wait for the two of us to settle into your house and start a family."

"Like I told you, I'm not the same man I was then."

"People don't change that fast."

"Oh? What's the acceptable rate, in your opinion?"

"You're getting sarcastic, again."

"No, really, what is the usual timeline for personal change? For all I know, I've set a record for accomplishing it in under three months."

"You know what? We're not getting anywhere with this discussion."

"Argument."

"Whatever it is, I vote we table it."

"I vote we table it until we're in bed. We've never had an argument in bed. I want to see what that's like. Could be interesting."

Doggone it. She had a weakness for his sexy talk. She had a weakness for *him*, full stop. "That's a really bad idea."

"No, it's not. We could kiss and make up."

It sounded lovely. Too lovely. In her present mood, she didn't trust herself to—

"Unless you're afraid." Again, the words came softly.

Her heart raced. "I'm *not* afraid." She grabbed a chunk of reality and leaned on it. "It's just that tomorrow's a big day. I need to be on my game."

The silence filled with the soft clop-clop of the horses' hooves.

"Okay, Val."

29

Teague didn't sleep very well, mostly because Val didn't, either. Instead of repeating the spooning that had worked like a charm the night before, she'd claimed the night was too warm for it.

Yeah, not so much. He'd left the window open about an inch and the breeze coming through it had been downright chilly. Clearly she'd had no interest in cuddling.

He'd stayed on his side of the bed while she'd moved around restlessly on hers. Eventually she'd slept, but fitfully. Muted sounds of distress had jerked him awake on a regular basis.

As he stared into the darkness while she struggled with her dreams, he had ample time to regret his words on the trail. Zeke's comments followed by a terrific outdoor experience had made him bold. And optimistic that he'd get a different response on the timing thing.

When he hadn't, he'd allowed frustration to take over. Always a mistake, and more so in this case. Because maybe, just maybe, Zeke was right. Her reaction could mean exactly that. But instead of calming her fears, he'd stirred them up. *Way to go, Sullivan.*

Eventually the sky turned pearly gray, signaling the end of the tortuous second half of the night. His fault. All his fault.

"I'll jump in the shower if you'll start the coffee."

He turned his head. She lay on her side, looking at him. He rolled to face her, his chest tight with remorse. "Val, I'm so sorry. I behaved like an idiot."

"I'm sorry, too. I should have spent the night at my house."

"And miss the cowboy cookout?"

"I wouldn't have known I was missing it. You only thought of it because I decided to stay."

"But aren't you glad you did? Even though I screwed up the ending, you discovered that camping's super important to you. Now you can—"

"I'm grateful to you for that. I'm grateful to you for a lot of things. And I'm not being very nice to you in return."

"What are you talking about? You agreed to this whacky idea of a fake engagement. I'm hugely in your debt for going along with an idea you initially hated."

"No, I didn't."

"Val, you came unglued. You yelled at me. You demanded I call my mom on the spot and tell her the truth."

"Well, sure. Because it was a totally insane concept. I couldn't imagine pulling it off, at least at first. But I didn't hate the thought of getting sexually involved with you. That was exciting."

"That's good to know. I didn't come up with the fake engagement just to get you back in my bed, but I'm sure that was one of the reasons why I thought of it."

"And here I am."

"Lucky me."

"Not really. Because every time we make love, you get your hopes up."

"That's not all I get up." He wanted a smile, just a little one. He got it. "Just trying to lighten the mood."

"I know. You've done an outstanding job of that this week."

"*We've* done an outstanding job. It's been a joint project."

"And Zeke is no help, planting the idea in your head that I'm falling in love with you."

"I shouldn't have told you."

"I'm glad you did so I know what I'm dealing with. I can see why he'd say it and you'd want to believe it. If I fall in love with you, I'm automatically on the right path."

"What path is that?"

"The one that leads to marriage."

"Doesn't have to."

"Maybe not for some people, but for you, it definitely does. You're a dyed-in-the-wool romantic just like your mom."

"You don't know me as well as you think you do."

She took a deep breath. "That's possible. But even if my assessment of you is wrong, I know myself better now, partly thanks to Ed's question about my parents."

"Ah."

"I'm terrified of ending up like that."

"I've reasoned that out."

"I may never get over it."

He let that sink in. Contradicting her wouldn't do much good at this stage and might do harm. "Understood."

"Even if I were falling for you, which I'm not, I'm the worst possible choice you could make."

He wanted desperately to argue the point, but she'd likely take it as more proof that he was a hopeless romantic who believed love conquered all. Which it did.

He cleared his throat. "Assuming that you're the worst possible choice, like you say, where do we go from here?"

"I don't know. We have a little more than two days left."

"And two nights." They were almost down to the wire. He ignored the ache in his heart.

"I'm not doing you any favors by having sex with you."

He managed a smile. "I wouldn't say that."

"Think about it."

"I do, all the time."

"We have yet to have bad sex or even mediocre sex. It would be helpful if we bombed out once or twice, but—"

"You think we should try to have awful sex?"

"I don't know how to do that."

"That makes two of us."

"But can't you see how this works? No wonder you keep asking to extend the time."

"Exactly. The mystery is why you don't agree."

"Because it's a dead-end street for you!"

"I don't care. I like this street. There are trees and flowers and butterflies here. And a whole bunch of amazing—"

"Look, we've debated this enough. Since I'm convinced great sex inspires you to ask for more time, and we can't seem to manage bad sex, the obvious answer is to cut out sex entirely."

"I don't care for that answer. Got any more?"

"Only one. Agree with me that Sunday is the end of it. Promise me you'll stop pushing for more."

His mood dimmed considerably, but the light in the room was brighter, now. Her expression left no doubt that she was serious. And she had a right to call the shots. He could either agree or sleep on the couch.

He dragged in a breath. "I promise. Sunday it is." Rolling over, he got out of bed and reached for his jeans. "I'll make coffee."

The kitchen was pretty much a mess. They'd bagged up the garbage, put that in the can outside and left the blue enamelware and utensils in a sink of soapy water.

The partially unpacked saddlebags hung over the back of a kitchen chair. The quilt lay on another one, the windbreakers on a third. The bag of cookies sat on the kitchen counter next to a row of empty cider bottles. They were rinsed out but hadn't made it to the recycling bin yet.

He'd deal with all of it later. Last night he'd suggested that Val skip helping him feed this morning. She'd insisted on doing it. Thanks to their pillow talk this morning, they were running late.

He could skip shaving and a shower so they'd get done feeding in time to come back here for breakfast. She'd need the protein since she hadn't had a good night's sleep.

His mom wouldn't have slept much, either, if the tales of those sleepovers were to be believed. Ed might have exaggerated some, but the Brotherhood had verified that bawdy karaoke sessions often lasted into the wee hours.

When the coffee pot quit gurgling, he carried a mug into the bedroom. Sweet-smelling steam drifted from the open bathroom door but the shower was no longer running. She'd be drying off, now.

Two more mornings. "Your coffee's on the top of the dresser. Thought you'd like to get a head start on it."

"Thanks!"

"Anything I can do?"

"You aren't going to shave?"

"I'll shave and shower later."

"Oh."

"Do you want me to shave?"

"No, I— never mind."

He wasn't in the mood for *never mind*. "What?"

"Either way is fine. You look sexy with the scruff but I love watching you shave."

Well, now. "Sounds like a win-win to me. I'll go with the scruff for now."

She laughed. "Okay."

"To repeat — anything I can do? I mean, anything that won't slow us down?"

"You could talk to Florence."

"Seriously?"

"No, she likes it better when you joke around."

"Val."

"I make it a practice to talk to her every morning, give her some carbon dioxide to start her day. If you'd do that, and check her soil to make sure it's moist, that would save me some time."

"You're putting me on, but I'm gonna do it."

"I'm not, either!"

"If you need anything else, I'll be in the living room chatting up Flo. Because I'm just that confident in my masculinity." Walking out, he continued into the living room.

"How're you doing, Florence?" He crouched down next to the coffee table and dipped his finger into the moist soil. "Good, I'd say." Lifting his finger, he brushed the black crumbs back into the pot. "You add a nice bit of color to this spot, by the way."

Florence just sat there looking green.

"Here's a funny story for you. Val brought you to help convince my mom that a woman lives here. She hauled a big pile of clothes over, too, for the same reason. And her regular shampoo and conditioner instead of a travel size. A few romance books, too, which she hasn't cracked. I was hoping she'd read one of them to me. Especially the juicy parts."

Florence didn't so much as turn a leaf. Her expression remained epically serene.

"I wonder why she reads romance. Do you know? Given her views on the matter, I'm not sure it makes sense. But there you have it."

He gazed at the plant. "Here's the punch line to that long story. My mom hasn't set foot in here. You'd think she'd be eager to see me cohabitating with a woman at long last. You'd think she'd have dropped several hints about it. Nope."

Flo said nothing.

"See? You can't explain it, either. True, we've been busy, but still... I would have expected her to come up with a reason to scope out—" He glanced up as Val walked in carrying her mug of coffee. "Flo and me, we're shooting the breeze."

She smiled. "I could hear you. Good job."

"She's a great listener. I was just telling her that we added all these things to the house for my mom's benefit and she hasn't seen any of it."

"I thought of that yesterday. I offered to pick her up and I honestly expected her to suggest walking down here. It would have been a golden opportunity to get a peek at our living arrangements."

"I'm kinda glad she didn't suggest it, to tell the truth. We've got stuff scattered all over the kitchen."

"I know." She polished off her coffee and headed into the kitchen with her empty mug. "Let's get a move on so I can help you clean up before I leave."

"Nah, I've got it. I'm more interested in cooking up a nice breakfast so you'll have plenty of energy for those munchkins." He grabbed his hat and ushered her out the door.

"Are you still planning to oil the saddlebags this afternoon?"

"Are you still in the mood to help me?"

"Yes, I am."

That gave him a lift. "Then we'll do it."

She put on her hat as she walked down the porch steps. "I'm losing track. Is anything scheduled for tonight?"

"When Ed told me they were staying at the Buckskin for the sleepover, she said to plan on a quiet dinner tonight at her house followed by an early bedtime for the two of them."

"Do you think your mom will be up to going to my school today? I hate to drag her along if she—"

"You couldn't keep her away. She lives for stuff like this. Besides, after the girls cheered when they heard she was coming, she'll guzzle as many energy drinks as necessary to be present for those kids."

"Alrighty, then."

"Gonna read me a romance book tonight?"

She gave him a long look. "Why?"

"I've always been curious about what's in them."

"Romance."

"Shocker."

"And if you're wondering why someone like me, who has issues with the whole love and marriage deal, is reading romance..."

"It crossed my mind."

"If you'd asked about it a few days ago I'd have said I like the historical detail, but they're not all set in the past, so that doesn't hold water. I might have said I like reading about places I've never been, but that's probably a copout, too."

"Then why are you reading them?"

"Therapy."

30

On the way to pick up Tatum and Piper, Madeline regaled Val with some of the doings of the sleepover. "I cleared all this with Ed before telling you. I didn't want to reveal anything I shouldn't."

"I think by now everyone knows about the bawdy karaoke songs. Adding tap dancing to the karaoke shouldn't surprise anybody."

"I had a blast. A couple of them could become decent tappers if they choose to practice. Unfortunately, they want to dance to those bawdy songs, which means no public performances."

"A new twist to *Dirty Dancing*."

"No kidding. Loved that movie. To think you weren't even born when it came out."

"But I've seen it. The eighties had a lot of good movies. I love just about everything John Hughes directed."

"Me, too! We should binge-watch John Hughes movies sometime."

"Sounds like fun." She wasn't making that up, but she couldn't see it happening. There was a better chance of the Babes tap dancing to bawdy songs in public.

"What did you and Teague do last— oh, never mind. That's nosy. You don't have to tell me."

"I can tell you. We took Nugget and Silver for a trail ride and had a cowboy cookout in a meadow by Crooked Creek."

"What a great idea. There was even a full moon."

"Yep." Too bad they ruined the ambiance with an argument.

"He loves being outdoors. Naturally I was hoping he'd decide to teach, but I learned pretty quick that he'd hate being stuck in a classroom."

"But he is teaching as a sideline."

"And I was proud as punch watching him yesterday. He has a kind, gentle approach. Aren't the riding lessons how you two met?"

"Yes."

"And you were a beginner?"

"Very much so."

"You don't look like one, now. I'd like to claim it's because Teague's an excellent teacher, but I'm guessing you have some natural abilities."

"Evidently I do. It was a complete surprise to me."

"But it's no surprise you and Teague hit it off right away. Ed told me he jumped the gun with the proposal and I thought *déjà vu all over again*. Wes did the same thing. Only difference is I said yes. My parents had a fit but I defied them. We went full speed ahead, damn the torpedoes."

"I guess I'm more cautious than you."

"I'm not advocating that approach, believe me. We didn't know each other well at all. Our marriage could have been a total disaster. We lucked out."

"I'm glad." How interesting Madeline viewed it that way since her husband died so young.

"Before we pick up Tatum, I wanted to throw something out there."

"Sure." Her gut clenched. "But we're only about three minutes from her house." Was Madeline going to challenge the authenticity of this engagement *now*? Lousy timing if she was.

"This won't take long."

"Then go for it."

"When I was teaching fulltime, my buddies and I had a tradition when we set up our rooms and I miss it. But you don't have to do this to please your future mother-in-law. It's just an idea."

Val relaxed. Not about the engagement. "Let's hear it."

"About five of us would organize our rooms on the same day. When we finished, we'd cue up Gloria Estefan on somebody's phone. Then we'd form a conga line and dance up and down the hall. Usually we grabbed a few more teachers along the way. Do you think the girls—"

"Would love it? That's a no-brainer. Since you're the one with the dancing credentials, you should teach them to conga. I predict it'll take about thirty seconds."

"Yippee! I thought of this on the drive over from Eugene and hoped you'd like it. Having kids involved will make it even more fun." She gave Val a glance. "I see you ditched the bandana."

"I don't expect to sweat, so makeup does the trick."

"Coming up with bandanas for everyone was very creative."

"I have my moments."

"You're a talented lady, Val. It's easy to see why Teague is smitten." The words were lovely and the tone kind.

Guilt swamped her. "Thank you. I think he's great, too."

* * *

Val called for a vote before they started. Nell's room first or hers? It was unanimous. Nell's, or rather Miss O'Connor's, would be first because third grade came before fourth.

Nell and the girls reminisced as they worked. Remember when Shayla knocked over the bottle of glue and the floor was sticky for days? When Tony brought his pet mouse for show-and-tell and it got loose? When Riley brought one of Mister Rogers' shoes, dropped it on Miss O'Connor's foot and broke her little toe?

Val didn't mind the walk down memory lane that didn't include her. Her epic adventures with these precocious kids were ahead of her, waiting to be discovered.

Spending the summer sharing riding lessons with them would make the school year even richer. Teague was right. She had to continue those lessons, for her sake as well as theirs.

Setting up her room always started with the music that would go with each area of study.

Last night's ride had inspired her to switch things up a bit and start with her Native American unit. *Red River Valley* was one of the cornerstones.

Last year she'd used tea to create a page that looked old and calligraphy to hand-write the lyrics. The girls were fascinated.

"I love this writing." Piper traced it with a finger. "Can we learn this?"

"The song or the calligraphy?"

"I wanna learn *both*." Riley spread her arms wide.

Claire studied the words. "There's a story here."

Val smiled. "Indeed there is. More than one is connected to this song."

"We could make a play!" Tatum hopped up and down. "Can we make a play out of it, Miss Jenson?"

"Great idea."

"A *great* idea." Riley twirled around. "We can do it on stage in the *auditorium*. Auntie Madeline, you have to come for it!"

She chuckled. "Of course I do. Just let me know the date and I'll be here in a flash." Moments later, when the girls were discussing which color pushpins to use, she moved closer to Val and lowered her voice. "Teague does a nice version of this on the harmonica."

"I know."

Madeline brightened. "He played for you?"

"He did. I gather the harmonica is somewhat of a private talent, but if I could get him to perform it for the class, that would be—"

"Who plays the harmonica?" Claire appeared out of nowhere.

"Um..."

"It's Uncle Teague, isn't it?"

"Yes, but—"

Nearby, Nell glanced her way and lifted her eyebrows in surprise.

Claire crossed her arms and huffed out a breath. "He never told me. Why not?"

"He's kind of private about it," Madeline said.

"But he could team up with Uncle CJ."

"Who could?" Riley came from the far side of the room, followed by Piper and Tatum.

"Uncle Teague plays the harmonica, but you can't tell *anybody*. It's a private thing."

They all nodded solemnly.

"Except a harmonica goes great with a guitar. Uncle Teague and Uncle CJ would be so cool together. I'm gonna talk to him about it."

Val put a hand on her shoulder. "Not everybody wants to be in the spotlight, Claire."

"I know. Everybody's not like me. My dad says that all the time." Her brow furrowed. "Okay, maybe not on the town square during the Labor Day celebration, but at least around the fire pit for the Buckskin gang. I know everyone would *love* that."

"She's right," Nell said. "Especially CJ. He'd get a charge out of having a sidekick. It does seem a shame not to at least mention it to Teague."

He might just need a nudge, like when one of the wranglers had coaxed him into it before. And he loved hanging out with the Brotherhood. "Then I'll say something to him."

Claire glanced up and smiled. "Good idea, Miss Jenson. He'd do anything for you."

Her breath hitched. Yes, he would. Anything at all. And that included walking away.

* * *

Val couldn't have asked for a better outcome. Her room looked great and the girls couldn't wait to start school and create their *Red River Valley* play. Madeline's conga line as a grand finale to the room prep was a hit.

Then lunch at the Moose turned into a celebration after Piper shyly mentioned that her birthday was the following week. Madeline insisted on paying for the entire meal and the chocolate layer cake.

Because nobody working that shift was adept at cake decorating, it appeared with candles and HAPPY BIRTHDAY, PIPER written on a sticky note attached to a skewer. She loved it.

After lunch, the girls piled into Nell's SUV for their overnight at the Buckskin. They'd spend the next morning braiding manes and tails in preparation for the riding demonstration.

As Val drove away from the Moose, she looked over at Madeline. "You must be bushed."

"I'll probably take a nap when we get back. But I wouldn't have missed any of this for the world. Thank you for including me."

"Of course! It's been a terrific day. I'll bet the conga line will turn into a thing at Apple Grove

Elementary. You might have to..." She caught herself before she said *come back for this next year.* "I don't think I have any Gloria Estefan tunes on my phone. You might have to show me which album to buy."

"As opposed to me coming back next year?"

"Um..."

"That's what you started to say, isn't it?"

She took a deep breath. "Yes, ma'am."

"Val, it's time."

Here we go.

"Please tell me what's really going on with you and my son. Starting from that first riding lesson."

Heart pounding, she nodded. Then she spilled her guts, leaving nothing out except the details of their lovemaking. Sometimes she had to stop and clear the guilty sadness from her throat.

Even though she didn't turn her head to look at Madeline, her peripheral vision gave her plenty of info. Teague's mom sat quietly, her gaze steady, her body language relaxed, the stance of a woman who was absorbing every word. Without judgment.

When the tale was finished, leaving Val drained and sweaty, Madeline put a hand on her shoulder and gave a little squeeze. "Thank you. That wasn't easy."

"No. But it's a relief. I hope you know how much Teague loves you. He just—"

"He went into self-preservation mode. I understand. I made *my* move because I sensed something was wrong. I heard it in his voice. Seeing him in person was the only way I could get to the bottom of it."

"Would you have moved here?"

"Oh, yeah. Not permanently, but I would have stayed until I'd figured out the issue and whether there was anything I could do about it."

"Clearly you've not blaming him. And I hope someday you'll forgive me for—"

"There was never any blame to start with. For him or for you. Maybe for me."

"Oh, Madeline, you were just—"

"I said *maybe.* I tend to be pretty easy on myself, too. I have plenty more to say on this subject, to both of you, but not now. I'm beat. We'll talk at dinner. Ed can referee."

"Will we need one?"

She smiled. "No, but she'll appoint herself to the position, anyway. She did last night at the sleepover."

"Why was she the referee at the sleepover?"

"We spent a good part of last night debating this situation. I already knew most of what you told me, but I wanted to hear it from you."

"Oh... my... God." She pulled up next to Ed's massive stone steps and turned to stare at Madeline. "You've been sitting on this all day?"

"The news last night didn't come as a surprise. I flat-out told them I doubted the entire setup and I was planning to ask you and Teague about it at some point today. They decided to prep me in advance to lower the temperature. Besides, they had some things to say on the subject."

"I'm stunned."

Madeline lay a hand on her arm. "Go rest up. Teague should, too. Ed and I will see you both at six."

"Okay." Val swallowed. "Will there be champagne?"

"Absolutely."

"Good."

31

Teague used Val's absence to practice doing without her. When he mucked out the stalls, he took off his shirt because the day was unseasonably warm. If a certain person who liked seeing him bare-chested wasn't around, her loss.

When he shaved, he had the bathroom to himself. If she was missing her eye candy, too bad. Didn't have to worry about the mirror fogging up, either. That was a good thing, right? It would be nice when the extra shampoo and conditioner bottles weren't cluttering up his shower.

Soon he'd have the entire dresser for his clothes. The whole closet, too. He'd lived alone ever since Ed had pared down to one wrangler and he'd been fine with that. Mostly. He'd be fine with it again.

He was used to eating meals alone, so having lunch by himself was like old times. Except he ate it way too early. He hadn't been particularly hungry after sharing a big breakfast with Val. But he'd run out of chores around the house so he'd made lunch.

The kitchen clock was not his friend. It told him Val wouldn't be back for at least three hours.

He'd carried the saddlebags down to the tack room but he couldn't start oiling them because he'd promised to wait for her.

After he cleaned up his lunch dishes and wiped down the counter and the kitchen table, he was officially finished with everything he absolutely had to do. Not good.

He wandered into the living room. "You know what, Flo? After you go back home, I'm getting somebody just like you. I always thought having a houseplant was a silly idea and I'd probably kill whatever I brought in here."

Flo listened, like she always did, without comment.

"But if all you need is to be watered on a schedule and a little daily conversation, I can handle that. I'm not saying I can replace you. I realize you're special. But maybe I can find somebody who's similar but different, if you know what I mean."

Since she said nothing, clearly she did know exactly what he meant.

"Tell you what. Since Val might not get around to reading me one of those romance books, maybe I'll take a look at one now. Don't want to miss my chance to find out what's in them and time's running short."

His breath caught. He would have to go and say something like that. Ironic that he was stuck with extra time. After Val came back, he wouldn't have a single second to spare. Each one would be more precious than the rarest gem.

He was a third of the way through one of the paperbacks when Val walked in. He levered himself out of the cushy easy chair. "Hey, there."

"Hi." She put down her two canvas bags of supplies.

She didn't act particularly glad to see him. He squelched his first impulse, to go over and kiss her hello. Instead he held up the book. "Have you read this?"

"Yes."

"Does the guy end up with the woman he's crazy about?"

"Yes, he does."

"Whew, that's a relief. At this point things look bad for those two." He closed the book but left his finger in the spot where he'd quit reading.

"The couples always get together at the end of a romance novel."

"Always?"

"Yes. If they don't, it's not a romance."

"Interesting." Looked like this interlude with her would be disqualified.

He pulled his bandana out of his back pocket and laid it inside the book to mark his place. Then he left it on the coffee table next to Flo. "Do you want something to drink? We can take a couple of bottles of cider down to the tack room. That's assuming you still want to oil the—"

"Your mom knows everything."

Oh, boy. That was why she didn't look overjoyed to see him. The quick jolt to his system didn't last long, though. What difference did it make to the eventual outcome? "That's fine, Val. No worries."

"You're not upset? Or surprised?"

He walked toward her. "If I'd given myself time to think about it, I could have anticipated this. My mom's very persuasive."

"She didn't have to coax me. She asked what was actually going on with us. I told her. Turns out she knew most of it already. It came out at the sleepover."

He paused, disconcerted. "The Babes blew our cover?"

"She let them know she planned to ask us some questions today because something was fishy. They decided to disarm the bomb."

"Oh."

"They made the right decision. She had time to process it before she saw either of us. And wow, does she have self-restraint. She kept it all to herself until we were driving back. It didn't impact the special time with the girls one tiny bit."

Now that he was only a few feet away, he picked up on the fatigue in her eyes. She'd been on the front lines while he'd been home reading a book. Time to get his head out of his butt.

Closing the gap, he drew her into his arms. "I'm a jerk. I should've figured out it would go that way. If I'd told her the whole story before she got involved in the sleepover, then you wouldn't have had to—"

"I'm *so* glad you didn't do that! Think of what it would have been like for me and your mom today if you'd confessed yesterday."

He took a breath. "Bad."

"Very bad. Even if we'd kept a lid on it for the sake of the girls, they would have picked up on our stress and the whole plan would have been compromised."

"In other words, I put you in a lose-lose position. What a guy."

"It wasn't lose-lose." She cupped his face in both hands. "We had a wonderful day. The kids had a ball. Your mom taught them to conga and after we were done, she led a conga line down the hallway. A couple of other teachers joined in. Harland Kuhn came out of his office and danced with us."

"She did the conga line when she was fulltime at her old school."

"She told me. I anticipated having fun today, but I didn't know she'd be one of the best parts of it."

"Even though the ride home was hell?"

"It was rough, but liberating. I felt so guilty trying to convince her I'm something I'm not. I'm glad that's over."

Then it dawned on him. "And you can go home."

She blinked. "I didn't think of that."

"No? I would have expected it to be the first thing you thought of." His whole body began to ache. "Want me to help you pack up?"

"I can't leave yet."

"Why not? Party's over." God, this hurt.

"We're invited to have dinner with your mom and Ed up at the house."

"Why?"

"Your mom has some things she wants to talk to us about. But she was exhausted when I dropped her off. She plans to take a nap so she'll be ready to tackle whatever deep discussion she has in mind."

"Are you sure she needs both of us? You've already been put through the wringer. I can handle this by myself. My problem. My job."

"Trying to get rid of me?"

That stopped him in his tracks. "I thought you wanted to go."

"I do, but..."

Confusion rattled in his brain. "Is it the saddlebags? I have a hard time believing you're stalling so you can help me with them, but—"

"That's not it. I'd like to go to dinner tonight and hear what your mom has to say about all this. She's not angry, Teague. She's... processing."

He nodded. "She does that."

"I admire the way she's reacted. No drama. Tons of empathy. This is going to sound sappy, but I want to be her when I grow up."

"Then we'll go to dinner. And oil the saddlebags between now and then." Maybe after dinner she'd load up her truck and drive away. Or maybe she'd stay one more night. He'd take it as it came.

"Although I asked to help you with the saddlebags, I'm afraid I might nod off in the middle of it. I didn't sleep much last night. I'm tempted to follow your mom's lead and take a nap instead."

"You've already put in one heck of a day. By all means, grab some shut-eye."

"I'll make a wild guess that you didn't sleep much last night, either. I woke up once and caught you staring at the ceiling."

"Sleeping with my eyes open. That's a thing."

"Baloney. I kept you awake, didn't I?"

"Maybe."

"Look, I don't want to fool around, but—"

"Oh, me, either." Although it might be his last chance.

"I'd like to make you a deal."

"The answer is yes."

"You don't know what I'm going to say."

"I don't care what you're going to say. Whatever it is, I'm down with it."

"Then see what you think of this. First we take a nice nap. No sexy times, but we could do that spooning thing if you're willing. It relaxes me."

Well, at least it was true for one of them.

"I was just being difficult last night because... well, you know why."

"You had a burr under your saddle by the name of Teague?"

"You didn't mean to be a burr."

"Oh, I think I did. I was prickly. But I'm better, now."

"I can tell." She smiled. "The nap works for you?"

"Yes, ma'am." A platonic bit of spooning with Val beat the heck out of oiling saddlebags.

"Then after our nap, we'll head up to Ed's house to have dinner and a discussion with your mom."

"So far so good." He held his breath. She was coming to the edge of the cliff.

"Then after dinner...."

He waited, chest tight.

"We'll come back here and go at it like bunnies."

He choked on a laugh.

"You okay?"

He cleared his throat, giddy with relief. "Yes, ma'am. I did *not* expect that phrase to come out of your mouth."

"Are you good with the plan?"

"Like I said before, the answer is yes. No, let me amend that. *Hell, yeah.*"

"It would be stupid to pack up and drive home tonight."

"I agree." It was only a short reprieve, but he'd take it. Loosening his hold, he slipped his fingers through hers and started toward the hall. "Let's get started on that nap. If we follow your plan, we'll need to be well-rested."

32

Val kept her clothes on except for her boots. Teague did, too. About thirty seconds after she nestled into the solid curve of his body, she was asleep.

She woke up disoriented. Why was she lying in Teague's bed fully clothed? Oh, yeah. The nap. Spooning.

Except he'd switched his position. He was still in the bed, but not spooning her anymore. And what was that whispery sound that came every so often? Ah. Pages turning.

Reaching behind her, she touched the denim of his jeans and the muscular calf under the material.

"Trying to feel me up, lady?"

"I couldn't figure out what you were doing."

"I'm riding hell-bent-for-leather toward the ranch where a slime-ball named Buck has my girl. If I don't get there in time, he's liable to—"

"That's the exciting part." She rolled to her back and patted his leg. "Keep reading."

"Okay." He moved his leg slightly, tucking it more firmly against her side as he turned another page.

Resting her arm on his knee, she cupped the swell of his calf muscle under the wear-softened material. This cozy companionship, a complete one-eighty from heavy breathing and hot sex, was slightly unnerving. Sweet, though.

When she'd asked for quiet time, a break from their usual passionate encounters, he'd given her that. Instead of rousing her from sleep with kisses and coaxing her to make love, he'd fetched the book he'd started earlier.

That floaty sensation was back, even though they weren't kissing or gazing into each other's eyes. Was this happiness? Whatever it was, she liked it.

If she stayed with Teague long enough, she might begin to believe the happily-ever-after in those books was achievable. But gaining that confidence could take months, even years. How long would she hold her breath, waiting for life to lose its luster?

He wanted kids. Would she ever have the courage to go that route? What if her parents had stuck together for the sake of her and her sister? What if they'd created a groove of routine so deep they couldn't climb out, even though their children had moved on?

Teague closed the book with a sigh. "Nice."

"You liked it?"

"What's not to like? Two good people who deserved to find happiness. And in the end, they did." He laid the book on the nightstand and gazed at her. "Processing?"

"Yes."

"Since you're not leaping on me and smothering me with kisses like the lady in the book, I won't ask questions."

Her heart stuttered. "Teague, I wish—"

"Me, too." He picked up his phone. "It's five-thirty. What time are we due at Ed's?"

"Six. And I'd like to take a quick shower before we go."

"Then I'll leave you to it." He swung his legs over the edge of the bed and stood. "I'll wait in the living room. Might start another book." He walked out.

So much for the floaty sensation. Sadness took its place. Soggy, drippy, cold sadness. She hated that he was unhappy. Her plan for after dinner could be a gigantic mistake, temporary pleasure that only made the pain worse later.

By the time she joined him in the living room, she was convinced they should cancel that part.

He marked his place in the book, laid it on the coffee table and stood. "You look terrific."

"Thank you, but I don't feel terrific. I feel like a louse. I shouldn't have made that deal with you. Coming back here for fun and games after dinner is a mistake."

"I'd suggest the meadow, but I don't think the venue is the problem."

"I've tortured you enough. I should just leave."

"I don't want that and neither do you."

"It's for the best."

"That's debatable." He picked up his phone and glanced at the time. "We need to go." He laid it back down and gestured toward the door. "After you."

She walked out ahead of him and waited at the bottom of the steps.

He settled his hat on his head as he came down to meet her, his gaze steady. He'd never looked better. She ached to go to him, wrap her arms around his solid warmth and be enclosed in his strong embrace.

He reached for her hand and laced his fingers through hers. "It'll be okay." Giving her hand a squeeze, he started up the hill, shortening his normal stride.

He'd been doing that all along, but tonight it touched her more deeply. Their time of walking hand-in-hand was coming to an end. Instead of chatting as they usually did, they climbed the hill in silence.

Madeline must have been watching for them because she opened the door as they stepped up on the porch. She glanced at their clasped hands, looked up and smiled. "I'm glad you're here. Ed's pouring the champagne."

Champagne. Teague was permanently linked to it, now. Champagne was only the beginning of a long list of reminders she'd be dealing with on a regular basis. He'd be in the same fix, only worse. He might have to remodel his whole house.

He let go of her hand and gave his mom a hug. "I'm sorry, Mom. I—"

"Now, now, none of that." She hugged him and patted his chest. "We'll get this sorted out. Come on in so we can get settled."

After Teague left his hat on the rack by the door, Madeline ushered them into the dining room where a crystal chandelier above the table cast rainbows over the snowy tablecloth. Enough shade had fallen on the walled garden outside the window to trip the switch for the fairy lights.

Candles and a flower arrangement signaled Ed's intention to make the occasion festive. Silverware and china gleamed. A flute filled with golden champagne sat at every place. The seating arrangement was two places on one side of the long table, one on the end and one on the opposite side.

Ed came out of the kitchen carrying a silver ice bucket with a fresh bottle uncorked and ready to deploy. Val appreciated her efforts and she looked forward to whatever wisdom Madeline chose to impart. But there weren't enough flowers, fairy lights and champagne in the world to turn this dinner into a celebration.

"Welcome, welcome." Ed put down the ice bucket. "Have a seat, please. You two take the chairs facing the garden. I sent my cook home again, so—"

"Then I'll help you serve," Teague said.

"No, son, I'm helping her." Madeline gestured toward the table. "Sit down, please."

Teague frowned. "But—"

"Sit down, please." Madeline smiled, but her tone was pure teacher-in-command.

"Yes, ma'am."

"We'll be right back." She whisked out of the room behind Ed. A sound that could have been a giggle came from the kitchen.

A gleam of amusement chased the shadows from Teague's gaze. He lowered his voice. "I think we're about to get a talking-to."

"Looks like it," she murmured. "We'd better sit down before we land in even more trouble."

"Yep." He pulled out the chair to his right and helped her into it. Then he took the one on the end and leaned in close. "I'm gonna guess my mom will sit across from us."

"Good guess. You notice the flowers and candles are to our right so they don't block her view."

"Saw that."

"She said Ed would referee, so putting her on the end makes—"

"Referee?" His volume went up. "Why do we need—"

"Ed's idea." His mom came out of the kitchen carrying two salad plates in one hand and a basket of fragrant dinner rolls in the other. "I told her it wasn't necessary."

"It sure isn't." He left his seat and relieved her of the salad plates. "I take full responsibility for this entire mess. If I'd told you at the start that moving in with me wasn't an option instead of coming up with a fake fiancée, we wouldn't—"

"Hang on, there, son. We need to set some ground rules." She put the dinner rolls on the table and laid a hand on his shoulder. "First rule, stay seated. I know it goes against what I taught you, but just pretend you're back in my classroom."

"I don't understand why—"

"Ed and I will be up and down serving the various courses and we can't have you popping up to help or hold our chair every time we leave the table or come back in with food."

"That's for sure." Ed deposited a salad plate at each of the empty spots.

"But—"

"Please stay seated. If it makes you feel like a kid again, that might be a good thing. That's where everything started, anyway." She put pressure on his shoulder. "Sit."

Val pressed her lips together to keep from grinning as her big strong cowboy followed his mom's orders. When his mother and Ed pulled out their own chairs, he started up, then sighed and sat down again.

Ed raised her glass. "To mutual understanding."

Four champagne flutes met in the middle of the table. After Val touched hers to everyone else's, she lifted it to her mouth and took a healthy gulp. Some nights were made for sipping. This was not one of them.

Madeline put down her glass and looked over at Teague. "Son, I owe you an apology. I—"

"No, you don't. You had every right to ask to come and live with me. I'm your son. But my response should have been—"

"I'm not apologizing for that. I'd do it again. I'm apologizing for brainwashing you."

"Brainwashing? What the—"

"When your father died, I wanted you to have a positive, loving image of him. But I overdid it."

"Nothing wrong with that. I'm sure he was a great guy."

"But I didn't just make him a saint. I painted our marriage as perfect so naturally you wanted the same thing."

"You think I expect a perfect marriage? I'm smarter than that, Mom."

"I agree, but marriage is still your main goal in life."

"Was."

She blinked. "Was?"

"My goals have shifted." He glanced at Val. "Although maybe not soon enough."

Her throat tightened as she met his gaze, but she managed to get the words out. "I don't want you to shift your goals." She swallowed. "Especially not for me."

He stared at her in silence for a moment. Then he turned to his mom and Ed. "Would you excuse us, please?"

They both nodded.

He stood. "Let's take this discussion out to the porch."

She was more than willing. Pushing back her chair, she put her hand in his as he helped her up. The courtly gesture got to her every time. She'd miss it.

He threaded his fingers through hers as he led her through the house and out the massive wooden door. She'd miss holding his hand like this, too.

A cool breeze soothed her hot face as she stepped out on the porch. She heaved a sigh of relief. "Thank you for getting us out of there."

"Want to head back down the hill?"

"Not yet."

He took her other hand and drew her closer. "My mom's right. I used to be fixated on marriage. I'm sure she helped guide me in that direction."

"Which is *fine* and I—"

"I'm not headed in that direction, anymore. I want—"

"You haven't thought this—"

"I want to be with you, whatever that means. I don't need—"

"Maybe not now." She looked up, memorizing the shape of his nose, the curve of his lip, the arch of his eyebrows. "But those goals aren't dead and gone."

"Not dead, but not a priority. My priority is you."

"I don't want to be your priority."

"Too bad. You are."

She took a deep breath. "The goals you've shoved aside — they're good ones. You'll make a wonderful family man. A terrific dad. Your kids will never hear *I told you so.* That's huge."

He studied her for several long seconds. "You're not going to let it go, are you? No matter how many times I say—"

"*You* shouldn't let it go. I couldn't live with myself if you gave up—"

"It's my choice, damn it!"

"No, it's not. I'm taking it away from you. Goodbye, Teague." Freeing her hands, she started down the steps.

He came after her and caught her arm. "Don't do this."

"Let me go." She hardened her gaze and hardened her heart. "I don't want you on my conscience."

His grip loosened and he stepped back. The pain in his eyes made her flinch. She turned and ran. This time he didn't come after her.

33

Teague couldn't make himself go back inside. He sat on the porch steps, the cold stone biting through his jeans, numbing his ass. Fine with him.

Lights came on in his house. Lots of lights. Val would be a whirling dervish, throwing her belongings into the big suitcase and the many canvas bags she'd brought. The process wouldn't take long.

The dome light flashed in her truck. The big suitcase thumped as she lifted it into the back seat. She left the front door of the house and both truck doors open while she raced back and forth, coming out loaded down, tossing things into the truck and running back for another armful.

When she doused the lights in his house, the ache in his chest was so bad he started massaging the spot over his heart. Maybe hearts really did break.

Slamming the passenger door, she ran around to the driver's side, hopped in and started the engine. Seat belt! He'd lay money she hadn't fastened it. But she drove away at a decent pace.

Maybe she'd fastened the belt on the way. Fingers crossed.

He lost track of time. Could've been minutes before his mom came out. Could've been hours.

She sat next to him on the steps. "She's gone."

"Yes, ma'am."

"Ed and I watched out the window."

He nodded.

"She loves you very much."

"Yeah, right."

"You don't know that?"

"How would I know that? She's never said it."

"Sure she did. The day I met her. I asked if she loved you and she said yes."

"She was playing a part."

"I know, but she was telling the truth. I've been watching her ever since that first day, and there's no doubt in my mind. She's loved you from day one."

"I know that's wrong. She craved my body, but after I proposed, she couldn't wait to get rid of me."

"Because you scared her to death. The specter of her parents' awful marriage rose up like the Ghost of Christmas Future."

"I doubt it. Her sister's marriage, maybe. But Ed's the one who helped her really look at her folks' dismal situation."

"But she's known about it on some level. The truth lurked under the surface, affecting her view of relationships."

"I guess."

"Her parents present a good front and yet she knows better. Whenever she sees an apparently happy couple, she wonders if they're secretly miserable, too."

"And maybe nobody's happily married?"

"Bingo. When you proposed, you brought out every fear she has about falling in love."

"How can you know this? You weren't there."

"I listened to her tell me the story today on the way back. That story was packed to the brim with fear. And love."

"Does *she* know she loves me?"

"I doubt it. My guess is she can't let herself know it. She pretends it's mostly physical. She insists she has a crush, a silly reaction that will fade."

"Which is BS."

"Sure, but if she admits it's love, the next step is a commitment, most likely marriage."

"She said that once. I told her it didn't have to be."

"She still thinks it does. She's very traditional that way. If you're in love, then you commit to the person you love."

"She reads a lot of romance books."

"That could explain it."

"Dear God." He gripped his head in both hands. "This is a nightmare. Should I go after her? Try and talk some sense into her?"

"I wouldn't advise it. She'll have to figure this out on her own."

"And if she doesn't?"

"She will. She's going to miss you horribly. Like I said, she loves you. Being separated from you will be intolerable."

He took a shaky breath. "I can't speak for her, but it's already intolerable for me."

"It's not like you'll never see her again."

"But she'll avoid me whenever she can. She won't want to—"

"She'll have a tough time ignoring you tomorrow during the riding demonstration."

"The riding demonstration! Damn. I forgot all about it."

"She might have, too, considering how she tore out of here like her tail was on fire. Love tends to give you tunnel vision."

"The riding demonstration." He shook his head. "We were supposed to use that as a rationale for why we couldn't tell the girls about our engagement."

"To justify that decision to me?"

"Exactly. Telling them would mess with their concentration and they'd louse up the show. Then I forgot we were supposed to use that as our excuse."

"Just as well. I wouldn't have bought it, anyway. As it is, you've skated on the edge of insulting my intelligence."

"I know. The plan was doomed from the get-go."

"Except it worked like a charm."

He stared at her in disbelief. "How much champagne have you had?"

"Not much. Don't you see? If you hadn't roped Val into this scheme, the two of you could have gone on for months loving each other from a distance. Your fake engagement brought everything to a head. I'm proud to have been the catalyst that got you to this point."

"Mom! I'm in hell! Val's in hell! How can you be happy about that?"

"You had to get here before you had any hope of making progress in your relationship."

"You call this progress?"

"Yes, son. Yes, I do. Now come inside and eat some of Ed's delicious food. You'll need your strength for tomorrow. It'll be a big day."

"I'm not hungry."

"I know that. Eat something, anyway. It'll help you sleep."

He didn't argue with her mom logic, but she was wrong. Nothing would help him sleep. He'd probably have to take the couch, and even then, his chances were slim to none.

Over a meal he didn't taste that he washed down with expensive champagne he didn't savor, he talked with his mom and Ed about the riding demonstration at two the next afternoon.

He glanced at Ed. "Did Claire ask you about bleachers?"

"She did. Jake, Matt and Rafe are coming over at nine to disassemble them and haul them over there."

"Good. I'll help. I guess you two and I might as well head over in one truck, maybe around one-fifteen. We can all fit in mine."

"I won't be going with you and Ed. Cliff's taking me out to the Buckskin after our lunch and dropping me off."

"Who's Cliff and why are you having lunch with him?"

"The banker. I danced with him at—"

"Oh. Right. That seems a million years ago. He wants to pick your brain about how to organize a clothing drive, right?"

"That's the excuse he gave. I think he wants to get something started."

Teague jerked out of his fog. "*What?*"

"He's attracted to me."

"But you live in Oregon."

"It's not the far side of the moon. He travels for business."

"Are *you* attracted to *him*?"

"If I'm totally honest with myself, yes."

Ed smiled. "Attagirl."

"I'm... I'm... I don't know what to say, Mom."

"I'm sure you don't. You've never encountered this situation. I'm not so different from Val, when you get right down to it."

"I don't follow."

"I've been scared of getting involved with anyone because I'm traditional, too. I might fall in love and even consider marriage, which somehow seemed disloyal to your father."

"Wow." He scrubbed a hand over his face. "I feel like I'm in a wind tunnel with things flying at me from all directions."

Ed laughed. "Get used to it. The older you get, the faster the wind and the more flying objects."

"Thanks for the comforting words."

"Which reminds me. The Brotherhood and the Babes are hosting a party tomorrow night around the fire pit. Everybody's invited."

"Val?"

"I'm sure Nell will invite her. Don't know if she'll be there. CJ's going to play. It'll be fun."

"Sorry. I have to organize my sock drawer." Literally.

His mom frowned. "Don't you dare stay home. It would be a perfect opportunity to... oh! Did Val mention about your harmonica?"

"What about it?"

"Well, this is sort of my fault. Val will be teaching the kids *Red River Valley* and while we were working on the bulletin board for it, I let slip that you play a beautiful version of that song."

"I see."

"I was delighted to hear that you played it for her."

He'd file that under Painful Memory #6:45, which is about the time they performed their little concert. "So I did."

"Anyway, Claire latched onto the information and she—"

He groaned. "Let me guess. She wants me to play around the fire pit tomorrow night."

"Not necessarily tomorrow night, but sometime. With CJ. Val said she'd ask you about it. I guess she forgot."

"Then let's pretend that you forgot, too."

"Would you hate it so much?"

"No, I wouldn't. Eventually. Maybe. But now is not a good time."

"Or the absolutely best time."

"Look, Val might not even show up for that gathering, and even if she did, me playing the harmonica isn't going to—"

"It's one of the reasons I fell for your dad."

34

Val had forgotten Florence. On top of that, she'd forgotten to mention the harmonica. She'd told Claire she'd do it. After living with Teague since Tuesday night, she knew his schedule.

She pulled in a little after ten, when he was likely to be mucking out stalls. She'd rewritten the note to him multiple times and the latest version lay on the seat beside her.

It shouldn't have been hard to explain her three points. She was taking the plant. CJ would probably like to have him as a musical sidekick. She would be civil to him during the riding demonstration.

That was it, all she needed to communicate. She was a teacher, for God's sake, fluent in the language. Not today. The note was lame but it would have to do.

Adrenaline pumped through her system as she climbed the steps and crossed the porch. Taking a deep breath, she opened the door and walked in.

She came face-to-face with an unshaven Teague. "What are you doing here?"

"I live here. What are you doing here?"

"I forgot Florence."

"I noticed. So did she. Don't worry, though. I told her it was just an oversight and you didn't mean to hurt her feelings."

"Teague."

He shrugged. "She'll get over it."

"I wrote you a note." She held it out.

He kept his hands in the pockets of his jeans. "What's it say?"

"I'd rather you just read—"

"I'd rather you just told me. You're right here."

She met his steely-eyed stare. It was a disguise. His pillow lay on the couch where he'd likely spent the night. "I forgot to tell you something about your harmonica."

"Oh, that. No worries. Mom filled me in."

"Are you going to do it?"

"Who knows?"

"Okay, then. You've been asked."

"Is that all?"

"No." She looked away. She could only take so much of that intense stare. "I... um... promise to be nice to you during the riding demonstration."

"As opposed to what? You've never lost your cool in public. Why do you feel the need to reassure me? Did you take some nasty pills after you got home last night?"

She turned back to him. "I had hoped we'd be friends after this, but..."

"It's not in the cards, is it, Val?" His voice softened. "We have to either take it or leave it. No middle ground for the likes of us."

She gulped. "Guess not. Do you want this note?"

"No, thanks."

"Then I'll see you at the Buckskin." She folded it and shoved it in her jeans pocket.

"Yes, you will."

She turned and started for the door.

"Oh, Val?"

Pausing, she resisted the urge to look at him. "What?"

"Thanks for leaving the book I was reading."

"No problem."

"Can't wait to see how it ends."

She dragged in a breath. "'Bye, Teague."

"'Bye, Val."

She hurried out the door and stumbled down the steps. Climbing in the truck was a chore when her legs were shaking. It took her forever to get the key in the ignition.

She longed to gun the engine and fly out of there, but she took it slow. Sending up a rooster tail of dust would be disrespectful. She'd already done enough damage.

Halfway back to town, she looked at the empty passenger seat. She'd forgotten Florence. Again.

* * *

Heading to the Buckskin without three chatty girls in the truck added to the weirdness of the day. Val turned on the radio and quickly turned it off again. Listening to her thoughts wouldn't be much fun, but country love songs would be worse.

Her house was in shambles and she'd left it that way. Chaos suited her for the time being. But heaps of clothes everywhere had meant hunting for ten minutes before unearthing her orange bandana. The hickey had faded, but she'd be in big trouble if she showed up without that bandana.

The girls had looked forward to this day all summer. She'd concentrate on them, on their irrepressible spirit and their joy at being allowed to show off what they'd learned.

During the drive, she ran a mental video featuring each of those munchkins. Serious Piper riding her beloved Lucky Ducky. Tall, lanky Riley, proudly mounted on Mister Rogers. Tatum sitting pretty on Henri's barrel racer, Prince. And Claire, who could barely contain herself now that Cinnamon lived at the Buckskin.

Teague beat her there. He'd parked at the far end of the barn, no doubt to leave room for the other vehicles that would arrive soon. She pulled in next to his truck because it made sense.

A section of bleachers from Ed's arena partially blocked the view of the corral. The bleachers made it official — they were putting on a show. The girls' chatter and laughter drifted from the open barn door, followed by a deeper male chuckle. Teague.

She paused, suddenly short of breath. Could she do this? The brief exchange with him this morning had been tough, but when he interacted with those four girls, his appeal shot into the stratosphere.

She had no choice, did she? They were counting on her to be part of an event they'd remember for years, maybe even the rest of their lives. She would paste a smile on her face and—

"Hi, girlfriend." Nell came out of the barn, her expression worried. "Teague heard your truck. He asked me to come out and make sure you're okay."

"Oh." The tight feeling in her chest got worse. He'd listened for the sound of her truck so he could send aid when she arrived? Who did that? Who else would have that much empathy for someone who'd just handed them a pink slip?

"You're not okay." Nell took her by the arm. "Let's walk."

She nodded, falling into step beside her. "Where?"

"We'll go down the path that leads to the bunkhouse. It's shady. You can catch your breath."

"Listen, you need to go back. I see where you mean. I'll just wander a bit by myself until I settle down."

"I'll stay with you."

"But—"

"Everything's under control. The Brotherhood groomed the horses this morning and the girls braided all the manes and tails. But of course Henri came up with more ribbons so they're adding a few finishing touches."

"Henri's in there? I didn't see her truck."

"Teague stopped by and picked her up. If you want my opinion, she asked him to because Ed phoned her and suggested it. Henri has a very calming influence on people."

"Everybody takes care of everybody around here, don't they?"

"Yes, they do." Nell gave her a sideways hug. "And I won't lie. We're all concerned about you and Teague."

"Please don't worry about me. I'll be fine. I just hate that he's suffering. That's what gets to me."

"Funny, but he says the same about you. He's fine, but he's torn up because you're not fine."

"What makes him think that?"

"You forgot Florence for the second time."

"Did he bring her?"

"No, because she wouldn't do well sitting in his or your truck all afternoon."

"No, she wouldn't. So where—"

"Still at his house."

"You know, this is ridiculous, you having to walk me like an overheated horse." She turned around. "We're going back."

"If you say so."

"I need to be able to handle being around him. We're continuing the riding lessons."

"Good point. So here's a question. Will you come to the celebration at the fire pit tonight?"

"There's a celebration?"

"Everyone was in the mood, especially because of this riding event. The Babes and the Brotherhood are hosting. If you're serious about tackling this issue head-on, then you should come."

"I suppose Teague will be there."

"I imagine so. He and CJ are talking about doing a jam session."

"Really? He's going to play?"

"That's what I hear."

"That's wonderful. Good for him."

"Will you come?"

She gulped. Teague was making an effort. She could do no less. "Yes, I'll come."

_35_

Teague made the Buckskin gang promise to take tons of pictures during the event, both stills and videos. The hour went by incredibly fast and he barely had time to blink, but once he grabbed a second to scan the crowd and was gratified to see phones held high, recording the action.

He'd been worried about Val, but she came through like a champ, riding flawlessly and praising the girls during every short break. She and Nell had as much influence on the kids' excellent performance as he and Zeke. After a summer of close contact, all four adults were in tune and the girls picked up on that consistency.

The enthusiastic crowd loved the riding drills and they went crazy for the rope tricks. He'd intended to be part of the demonstration, but at the last minute he changed his mind. They were a unit with their color-coordinated ropes and bandanas. They didn't need him.

He found a good vantage point and pulled out his phone. After a minute of video, he put it away and simply watched, his heart full. At the climax, when they jumped through their twirling loops, the stands erupted.

They took their bows, broad smiles on faces pink with excitement. Then they broke ranks and ran to him, arms outstretched. He crouched down and gathered them close. "Love you guys."

A chorus of *we love you, too, Uncle Teague* got him a little teary-eyed. "Okay, now. Time for our grand finale."

He led them over to the staging area by the barn where Matt and Jake had been keeping everything moving smoothly. Val and Nell were already mounted.

He and Zeke gave the girls a boost up before climbing on their horses. Teague rode Thunder, Matt's black stallion, and Zeke was on King, the buckskin Charley used to ride. Both saddles were fitted with flag boots. Matt handed up Montana's state flag to Zeke and the Stars and Stripes to Teague.

He settled the pole firmly in the boot and glanced at the riders, sliding his gaze quickly past Val so he wouldn't freak out either her or him. But he made eye contact with each of the four girls. "We're gonna knock 'em dead, ladies."

Claire punched a fist in the air. "Yeah, baby."

Zeke laughed and shook his head. "Madison Square Garden, here we come." He met Teague's gaze. "Let's do this."

Teague grinned. "Yeah, baby." He nudged Thunder forward, moving from a walk to a trot as he and Zeke approached the gate, the flags rippling in the breeze. This was the only musical number, and CJ had been a good sport about setting up speakers for a four-minute gig.

When CJ got the signal from Zeke, he hit the switch and Aaron Tippen's *Where the Stars and Stripes and the Eagle Fly* poured through the speakers. Teague and Zeke broke into a canter and burst through the gate, flags streaming as they split apart, circling the corral.

Riley and Piper followed, cantering like pros as they split, too, Riley riding behind Zeke and Piper behind Teague. Claire and Tatum came in next, with Val and Nell the last two through the gate.

Then they began their weave, riders crossing paths, slipping between each other in a seamless ballet in time to the music. They'd messed it up a little in the dress rehearsal when they'd used a portable boom box. But this time, as if inspired by the resonance of CJ's sound system, horses and riders executed perfectly.

The crowd rose to its feet, cheering and clapping along with the music. Teague picked out his mom in the crowd and she blew him a kiss. He gave her a smile. She'd taught him to be resilient. He'd get through this.

The music built to a crescendo. The group of eight ended the weave pattern and lined up side-by-side with Teague and Zeke in the middle. Then they walked slowly toward the crowd, the line *almost* straight as the final words of the song filled the air.

Despite the music and the cheers, Teague managed to catch Piper's awestruck *wow*. She'd been the most nervous and reluctant of the four, but chances were good she'd be totally on board after this triumph.

He'd loved it, too. Solo performances weren't his thing, but team events like this, where he shared the success of the event with others... yeah, he was down with that.

He led the single-file parade out of the arena as the spectators continued to shower them with applause and shouted praise. Heady stuff. Was Val soaking it up, too? Did he dare congratulate her on a job well done?

What the hell. Nothing to lose, right? The staging area was a circus. Thank goodness the Brotherhood stepped in to deal with the horses, because the group of well-wishers turned out to be larger than expected.

As Matt came to take charge of Thunder, Teague lowered his voice. "Who are all these people?"

"A lot of them are the extended families of the kids. Nell expected the parents, of course, but evidently some grandparents, aunts and uncles showed up. Even cousins."

"Well, good. They worked hard and I'm glad they have that kind of support."

"Add in the Babes and anyone they might've invited, and Val and Nell's principal, and some of the other teachers, and you've got a big crowd. And you gave them a great show."

"Thanks. Thunder's a dream to ride. I know you've had to work with him."

"Sure have, but he's worth the effort. And he looks fancy out there."

"Yeah, he does. Thanks again for letting me ride him."

"Glad to." Matt led the black horse into the barn.

"You both looked fancy."

He turned and there was Val. She'd sought him out. Right on schedule, his pulse began to race. What did it mean that she'd come looking for him? Maybe nothing. Her expression was guarded.

"Thank you. You did a terrific job. Very smooth."

"It felt that way to me, too. Like everything clicked into place."

"Did you have fun?"

"Yes." Her smile was tentative. "I did." She took a breath. "Gotta go thank Jake for taking care of Sundance. See you later." She hurried away.

See you later? What the hell did *that* mean?

* * *

Val's *see you later* comment dogged him for the rest of the afternoon. Good thing he had a lot to do or it might have driven him crazy.

He helped dismantle the bleachers and loaded as much as would fit in the back of his truck. Nick and Rafe pitched in and used Rafe's truck to haul the rest to Ed's arena, where the three of them put everything together again.

He walked them back out. "Thanks for doing this. Those bleachers made all the difference."

"Happy to," Rafe said. "You'll be there tonight, right? CJ is counting on it."

"I'll be there."

Rafe took off his hat and mopped his brow with his sleeve. "How come we've never heard of you playing the harmonica?"

"I dunno. It just seems dopey to mention it, like I'm looking for an audience."

"Trust me," Nick said. "You'll have a very happy audience tonight. If you ask me, we need more harmonicas in country music. It just fits."

"I always loved the sound. I don't exactly remember my dad playing, but my mom says he used the harmonica to get me to sleep at night."

"Yeah?" Rafe smiled. "That's cool. Must be why you took it up."

"Well, that, and my mom gave me my dad's harmonica when she thought I was old enough to take care of it."

"That's even better." Nick clapped him on the shoulder. "Can't wait to hear you play, dude. See you later."

See you later. The words rang in his head as he hurried through his evening chores and hopped in the shower. Nick meant them literally, but Val might have been tossing the phrase out for no reason. Folks said it all the time, even when they had no plans to see that person they were leaving.

He could call Nell and ask her. She'd know. But that move was straight out of junior high. No, thanks. He'd take Ed and his mom to the celebration and have a good time, no matter what.

Although he hung onto that sentiment during the drive to the Buckskin, he broke out in a cold sweat when he pulled in and parked in front of the bunkhouse. A quick scan of the vehicles told him hers wasn't there. Disappointment lodged in his chest, a chunk of ice that was liable to affect his ability to play.

"I'm so excited to be doing this." His mom was in a stellar mood. Evidently her lunch with Cliff had gone well, although she hadn't elaborated other than saying they'd had a good time.

He'd been tempted to ask a few pointed questions. He hadn't. The concept was too new, too unsettling. Better to keep his mouth shut until he had a better handle on it.

After helping his mom and Ed out of the truck, he glanced back at the road as another pair of headlights bobbed along it. Nope, not her truck. That little six-cylinder was distinctive.

See you later.

He'd been a fool to think that meant she was coming to this shindig. A bottle of apple cider should dissolve that icy lump in his chest and allow him to do justice to the harmonica tucked in his shirt pocket. His mom would love hearing him play. That was worth a lot.

36

Muttering her favorite curse words, Val pulled to the edge of the dirt road. Not the very edge, though, because the bushes would scratch her paint job. Nothing like being late *and* lost.

What an afternoon! Soon after she'd arrived home from the Buckskin, Madeline had called to ask if she could borrow some romance novels to get in touch with her feelings about romantic love.

Sure, why not? Val had gone through her stash looking for the ones with the most feels, the best happy-ever-after endings. Three hours later, she'd had a stack of books for Madeline and a life-changing revelation of her own. Teague deserved to hear it ASAP.

But she'd rocketed way past the time she should have left for the celebration, a celebration she clearly wasn't going to find without help. Grabbing her phone from the passenger seat, she texted Nell.

I'm lost.

If luck was with her, Nell had her phone and wasn't so engrossed in the party that she'd miss the faint ping of a text.

The screen lit up. *Oh, Val, I'm so sorry you're hurting. I've been thinking about you. Want me to come? I can be there in thirty minutes. I can spend the night if you need me to.*

Val sighed. She must have been truly pathetic in June if Nell had jumped to that conclusion. *I'm not mentally lost. I'm physically lost on this &%#@ ranch. Don't they believe in lights? Or signs?*

Where are you?
I DON'T KNOW.
Have you passed Henri's house yet?
4 times.
Go back to Henri's house. I'll talk you in from there.

OK.

With some tricky maneuvering, she turned the truck around and got back to Henri's driveway. Henri's porchlight and the one on the cottage nearby were the only beacons in the inky night. Clouds covered most of the stars. The moon wasn't up yet.

Although she'd driven to the barn dozens of times, she hadn't even managed to find that road. Her guidepost was a pine tree with a broken branch. Damned if she could pick out that tree from all the others, let alone the branch. Twice she'd turned on what looked like a road but was only a break in the trees.

Her phone chimed with Nell's ring. She snatched it up. "Thank God. This place is darker than the inside of a whale."

Nell laughed. "You've been inside a whale?"

"I saw *Pinocchio*. How do people navigate around here?"

"Did you use your high beams?"

"Yes, and I saw an effing *bear*. Scared the stuffing out of me, so I cut the brights and locked the doors."

"The bear's not a problem unless you have food in the truck."

"Nope."

"The meal's over, but I'm sure Jake will get you something."

She didn't give a flip about eating. Not after she'd finally figured out what she was feeling, what she wanted. But she'd wasted precious time. "I don't need any food. Please tell me I haven't missing the whole damned thing because I've been driving around for hours."

"Hours?"

"Twenty minutes."

"Are you sitting in front of Henri's?"

"Yep. Pointed toward the road that goes out of here."

"Turn around and go a quarter of a mile. Watch your odometer."

"Got it." By using the lower part of Henri's drive, she made the turn without having to back and fill.

"I'm glad you're here. When you didn't show, I was afraid you'd rethought it."

She had. Several times on the way home from the Buckskin. But after going through those books, she'd finally realized the four horsemen of the apocalypse wouldn't keep her away from seeing Teague tonight. "Not anymore. Just lost." She glanced at the odometer. "Okay, it reads a quarter of a mile."

"Turn on your high beams, look to your right and inch along until you see a road. It's close."

"Omigod! There it is!"

"That's the one to the bunkhouse. When you get there, you'll see a bunch of trucks in front. After you park, go around the left side of the building and there's a lighted path to the fire pit."

"Sounds doable."

"It's easy. By the way, if Henri acts weird when you talk to her, she's freaking out a little. She got a letter today from some guy claiming he's related to Charley Fox."

"Her late husband?"

"Right. I'll see you in a bit."

"Thanks, Nell. Oh, wait! Is Teague playing?"

"Yes, he is." She disconnected.

Val left the high beams on as she drove along a curvy dirt road. Eventually lights from the bunkhouse gleamed through the curtain of trees and she cut the brights. Didn't want to blind anybody who might be in the parking area.

Locating Teague's red truck, she parked as close as possible without blocking anyone. She switched off the engine and opened her door to... music. Guitar and harmonica blended with a voice she recognized as CJ's.

He'd performed during this summer's Fourth of July event on the square. She'd hung out with Harland and his wife Alice, taking care to avoid the Buckskin gang because Teague had been with them.

Those days were over... for good.

Trembling with anticipation, she climbed out of her truck and headed for the left side of the bunkhouse. The music and a faint glow in the sky guided her as she walked toward the back of the building.

Her breath caught. No wonder everyone raved about these gatherings. The large rock fireplace created a welcoming glow and projectors sent colored lights drifting through the trees. Candles flickered on the long picnic table and Adirondack chairs formed a wide semi-circle facing the fire pit. Some people sat there, but most were dancing in the large space between the chairs and the fire.

She hurried down the lantern-lit path, eager to get a glimpse of Teague playing, but the dancers blocked her view. The song ended amid laughter and applause. She still couldn't see him.

Then Jake turned in her direction. "Hi, there, sunshine! Hey, everybody, Val's here!"

"Hi, guys!" She moved into the friendly sea of folks who'd pitched in to make the riding demonstration a success. "Sorry I'm late. I got *so* lost."

"Lost?" Teague appeared, his smile welcoming but wary. "Why didn't you call me?"

Ah, the floaty sensation. She met his gaze and joy filled every part of her body. She wanted it to fill every part of him, too. "I texted Nell. I didn't want to interrupt your—" She gestured to the harmonica in his hand. "You sounded wonderful just now."

"Thank you."

CJ slung his guitar strap over his shoulder. "Teague's the missing piece. I don't know how I played without this guy. We're making magic tonight."

"I believe you." The group gathered around them fell silent. Clearly she and Teague had become the center of attention.

And she wasn't sure where to begin. She glanced at the harmonica in his hand. "Are you taking requests?"

"Yes, ma'am."

"We sure are!" CJ practically bounced. "We've come up with a whole playlist we have in common. We've got *Southside of Heaven,* we've got *Choctaw County Affair,* we've got—"

"Have you played *Red River Valley* yet?"

Teague's expression brightened a few notches. "No, ma'am."

"I'd like that one, please."

"You've got it." He stepped back and glanced at CJ. "You know the words?"

"Mostly. I might have to fake a few of 'em."

Teague looked back at her, eyebrows raised. "Would you—"

"I could sing if that's okay."

"Heck, yeah, it's more than okay," CJ chortled. "I'll gladly turn over the mic. Hey, everybody. Take a seat. We're having us a guest performance up here!"

"Dial it back, CJ," Jake called out. "You're gonna scare the lady."

Val sent him a smile. "It's okay, Jake. I'm not scared." Then she glanced at Teague and lowered her voice. "Not much, anyway."

The warmth in his eyes was worth the trickle of sweat running down her spine and the quiver in her stomach, which had nothing to do with the performance.

The group found seats in the chairs, on the chair arms or on the picnic benches. Madeline claimed a spot front and center. As her gaze locked with Val's, she smiled and gave a quick nod.

Val took a deep breath and returned her smile as the nervous trembling eased.

Bringing three musicians together without a run-through was crazy. Logically they should have fumbled the intro. Or messed up a bridge.

They didn't. She sang as if her heart depended on it. Teague put so much emotion into the wail of the harmonica that tears pushed at the back of her eyes every time she looked at him... which was often. CJ muted his contribution, strumming softly, letting them take the lead.

When they finished, a trance-like hush fell over the group. Then Jake shouted *hell, yeah!* and everyone leaped up and rushed forward to shower them with hugs and praise.

And congratulations? Somehow it became that, with the Brotherhood slapping Teague on the back and the women of the Buckskin gang hugging Val and wishing her happiness.

Teague gave her a questioning glance. Then he turned to CJ. "I need to take a—"

"Of course you do." CJ shooed him away. "Go, go. You two get out of here."

Teague tucked the harmonica in his shirt pocket, laced his fingers through hers and led her down the lighted path. "Do they know something I don't?"

"Nope."

"It's like they think—"

"That's on them. You'll be the first to hear what I have to say."

He paused. "You have something to say to me?"

She nodded and smiled.

His fingers tightened and he quickened his stride. "Can't wait."

"Where are we going?"

"To the parking area."

She was breathing hard by the time they rounded the building.

He swung around to face her. "I thought you weren't coming. But you did. I—'"

"Wait." She placed a hand over his talented lips. Then she caressed his cheek. "I need to tell you a few things first, please."

He sucked in a breath. "Okay."

"Your mom called me this afternoon."

His eyes widened. "What did you talk about?"

"Lunch with Cliff showed her she's out of practice with this romance business. She asked to borrow some of my books."

"Oh?"

"Does that bother you?"

"No. It's just... different."

"As I chose books for your mom, I started re-reading the part where the couple confesses their love for each other. I read a lot of those endings and finally... it sunk in."

His breath hitched. "What?"

She moved closer and slid her arms around his waist. "Teague, I'm so sorry."

"Sorry?" He stiffened.

She tightened her hold on him. "I'm sorry I couldn't tell you in June that I love you."

"June?" Then the second part kicked in. "You love me?"

"I do. But I didn't know it. I mean, I didn't let myself know because I was so scared of—"

His lips came down on hers, sweet at first, then more demanding, stealing her breath, pushing away all the words, making her dizzy with wanting him. She hugged him tight and kissed him back, pouring her whole being into telling him, showing him, how much he was loved.

He groaned and pulled her closer. A shudder rocked his body and he lifted his head, breathing hard. "I want to take you home. I need you so—"

"I think they'd forgive us if we leave."

"I hope so. I love you, Val. Love you with everything in me. I never thought I'd hear you say—"

"I love you, Teague Wesley Sullivan. I had this floaty feeling going on and I refused to admit what it was."

"You didn't want to love me?"

"I was *afraid* to love you. Big difference."

"But now..."

"I'm not scared anymore. Watching you at the riding demonstration today, thinking about what we've shared the past few days…. We could never ruin each other's lives. We're amazing together. It'll be so cool."

He smiled. "And hot."

"Oh, it was always hot. But now it'll be hot and cool at the same time." She hesitated. "But there's one thing I'm still pretty scared of."

"Getting married."

"Yes."

"That's fine. We don't ever have to—"

"I think we will. But could we just be in love for a while, let me bask in it and enjoy the sensation before we talk about getting married?"

"Absolutely. I promise I won't even bring it up. You tell me when and if you're ready. If that's never, I don't care, just so I'm allowed to keep loving you."

"Allowed and encouraged. And now I can return the favor." She gazed up at him. "We can't leave without telling somebody."

"My mom." He pulled his phone out of his pocket. "I'll text her." He started typing.

"Please tell her I'll give her the books in the morning."

"Yes, ma'am."

"And we can take my truck."

"Good idea. I'll leave my keys under the seat for her and Ed."

"Ask her to spread the word."

He laughed. "Probably don't have to tell her that, but I will." He finished the message and sent it.

The response was immediate. He turned the phone so she could see the string of hearts on the screen. "I think she's happy."

"That makes two of us."

"Three of us." He grinned. "Does this qualify as a romance, now?"

"Yes."

"Good, because we've been a major source of concern around here."

"And now we'll be a major source of joy." She grabbed his hand and slid her fingers through his. "Let's go home."

He tightened his grip as they hurried toward her truck. "You mean that the way it sounds?"

"Yes sir. Like it or not, you're stuck with me."

"And Florence?"

"That plant was never going anywhere. I knew she belonged with you. It just took me a while to figure out that I do, too."

"One more kiss for the road." Pausing beside her truck, he cupped the back of her head. "I love you."

She soaked the words up like liquid sunshine. "I love *you*." Her breath caught. "I can't believe how good it feels to say that."

"Feels even better to hear it." His lips gently touched hers.

And she was floating. Filled with an incredible lightness, she soared higher, carried aloft by happiness, joy, and most of all... love.

* * * * *

A mysterious stranger with a link to the past arrives at the Buckskin just in time for the holidays in GIFT-GIVING COWBOY, book ten in the Buckskin Brotherhood series!

* * * * *

New York Times bestselling author Vicki Lewis Thompson's love affair with cowboys started with the Lone Ranger, continued through Maverick, and took a turn south of the border with Zorro. She views cowboys as the Western version of knights in shining armor, rugged men who value honor, honesty and hard work. Fortunately for her, she lives in the Arizona desert, where broad-shouldered, lean-hipped cowboys abound. Blessed with such an abundance of inspiration, she only hopes that she can do them justice.

For more information about this prolific author, visit her website and sign up for her newsletter. She loves connecting with readers.

VickiLewisThompson.com

CPSIA information can be obtained
at www.ICGtesting.com
Printed in the USA
BVHW071222011122
650838BV00005B/208